Lam
The
FIC

D1046492

The Sugar Island

The Sugar Island

Ivonne Lamazares

HOUGHTON MIFFLIN COMPANY

BOSTON   NEW YORK   2000

Copyright © 2000 by Ivonne Lamazares
All rights reserved

For information about permission to reproduce selections
from this book, write to Permissions, Houghton Mifflin Company,
215 Park Avenue South, New York, New York 10003.

Visit our Web site: www.hmco.com/trade.

Library of Congress Cataloging-in-Publication Data
Lamazares, Ivonne.
    The sugar island / Ivonne Lamazares.
       p.   cm.
    ISBN 0-395-86040-7
    1. Cuban Americans—Fiction. 2. Miami (Fla.)—Fiction.
3. Cuba—Fiction. I. Title.
PS3562.A42175 S84   2000
813'.6—dc21   00-038917

Printed in the United States of America

Book design by Robert Overholtzer

QUM 10 9 8 7 6 5 4 3 2 1

FRANKLIN TOWNSHIP PUBLIC LIBRARY
485 De MOTT LANE
SOMERSET, NJ 08873
873-8700

For my mother, MERCEDES,
and for all my mothers;
For my daughter, SOPHIE;
For STEVE, without whom this
book would not exist

Acknowledgments

I have many people to thank for their friendship and support during the writing of this book. Thanks to Madrina and my grandparents for their love and example; to Padrino for knowing this book would be written years before I did; to my mother-in-law, Jan, for kvelling. My gratitude to my family at Miami-Dade Community College North, especially to Josett for her wise counsel; to Lou, Susan Orlin, Preston, Virginia, Robert, and others for ongoing encouragement. Thanks especially to Linda (1940–1999) for helping me change my life; to Elena Rosello for telling me her story; to Cecilia and Cary for years of friendship; to Ingrid for her loving care of our daughter. I am deeply grateful to Mary Morris for pulling the manuscript out of her student pile and helping to publish it, and for her invaluable feedback at every stage; to Russell Banks for his faith in me and generous support; to Wyatt Prunty and Cheri Peters for their kindness; and to the Sewanee Writers' Conference for providing a safe place to grow. Most of all, my thanks go to Gail Hochman, agent and good friend, who nurtured me and saw me through, and to Janet Silver, who patiently and lovingly edited the book in all its incarnations and in the fog of the writing process helped me to see. My love to Elena, with thanks for her ear and courage and for being "girls together." And to Steve, without whose deep and generous love, none of this would have happened.

You won't find a new country, won't find another shore.
This city will always pursue you.

— CONSTANTINE CAVAFY, "The City"

Everyone sees to it his fate is shared. Or tries to see to it.

— SAUL BELLOW, *The Adventures of Augie March*

Part One

1

Cáceres, 516 miles east of Havana, 1958

ONE DAY MAMÁ SAID life was about to start and ran off
to the mountains to become a rebel *guerrillera*. No one
knew exactly where she had gone until she came back
pregnant a year later on a burro.

My dog, Fyor, and I stayed with Abuelita Carmen — my
mother's mother — in her thatched *bohío*. From her porch
I searched the green hills for Mamá, Fyor barking beside
me. At night we'd fall asleep against a wooden post and
wake each morning on a cot in Abuelita Carmen's kitchen.

Mamá came back on a late afternoon in March, just
before my sixth birthday. Someone on a burro trotted up
the stone path and I knew it was Mamá. I hid in the guava
grove, shaking and covered with goose bumps. My belly
hurt. I squatted, pants down, and little worms rushed out
of me in a hot foam. I watched them crawl in my stool.
They had been eating me inside while Mamá was gone.

I stayed in the grove till sundown. By then the neighbors were sipping *café* on Abuelita's porch. Mamá had bathed and her hair dripped down the back of her housedress. I tripped over the porch steps but she caught me, lifted me high, my face against her throat, her words vibrating against my cheek.

She had stories to tell: El Che was a "beautiful man," Raúl Castro a "uniformed rodent," his brother Fidel a "Marxist-Leninist Opportunist." The fighting was moving west, Mamá said, away from Cáceres and the mountains. The rebels would be in Havana before the year's end. She looked at me. "But I'm glad I'm back."

Night frogs chittered in the brush as Mamá fell asleep in the rocking chair. Abuelita Carmen told everyone what they'd come to hear. She said her daughter "got knocked up by a rebel cook so they sent her home on a jackass." The neighbors nodded, some in sympathy. A few grinned. Then they went back to their shacks in the dark.

Sometime that night Mamá slid beside me on the cot. She moved her cold hands over my belly like she'd done at times back in Regla, when we lived by the harbor. But now I lay stiff, scared Mamá might get up and go back to her rocking chair on the porch. Now that she was a *guerrillera*, maybe she missed sleeping out with the crickets and the tough mountain wind.

The next morning Mamá told me all she would ever say about the rebel cook: "The path of a woman's heart, *mija*, is made slippery by hunger."

Abuelita Carmen frowned. But I thought about it; the path of Mamá's heart seemed slippery, regardless.

2

Regla, across Havana Bay, 1966

ON THE FIRST DAY OF SPRING, Mamá woke us, jostling her keys beside our heads. Before I could run to the cistern and wash my eyes she whispered, "Are you two my Storm Captains?" *The Storm Captain* was our favorite TV show.

My brother raised his arms and yelled, "Yes!"

"Well, captains," Mamá gave us a mock salute. "The high seas await us. Are we silent as—?"

"Tombstones!" We completed the question like Storm Captain sailors.

"If we're not silent tombstones we are—"

"Traitors!" Emanuel shouted and grabbed the stick he said was his sword.

It was so early Fyor still slept under his chair. On the kitchen table Mamá had spread a duffel bag and filled it with our baby pictures, cans of Russian meat, our rusty can opener, shirts, papers, plastic bottles of water.

"What is all this?" I asked.

On a corner lay a black-and-white picture of the three of us on Abuelita's doorstep in Cáceres, Emanuel then little more than a baby, leaning against Mamá, smiling.

I bit my callused thumb, pulled the skin with my teeth and chewed.

Mamá smiled. She loved to keep a game going.

"Your bracelet we'll hide in your underwear."

"Where are we going?" I asked louder.

"At midnight Cousin Romy from Cojimar will take us for a ride on his boat, *La Quintana*," Mamá said calmly, as if people took midnight boat rides for pleasure.

Emanuel asked if he could bring his sword. I fired off a list of questions like a detective about to catch someone in a lie. "What kind of boat is *La Quintana*? Why are we going at midnight? Is Fyor coming with us?"

"Storm Captains," was all Mamá said, "this is a long voyage." She stepped out onto the porch and lit a cigarette.

Emanuel smacked my shoulder with his sword. I wailed. Mamá did not look back.

At *siesta* time, Mamá leaned over the tin basin in the shade of our lime tree. The old ferry whistled behind us, lugging passengers across Havana Bay. Mamá poured a can of warm water over Emanuel's head and explained everything "for the last time."

She said I was thirteen years old and should have long ago reached the age of reason. "Remember El Gambao Casals?"

I didn't answer. Could anyone in this world forget their own father?

"A traitor, *mija. Un mierda.* Yesterday at the *bodeguita,* Castor and Richa from the crew got drunk and blurted it out. El Gambao defected." Mamá paused. "De-fec-ted," she enunciated, "as in he stayed in Panama."

Emanuel rubbed his eyes. Mamá dried his face with a scratchy towel.

Mamá had never married my father and after his trips abroad he only stayed in our Regla house for a week at a time, playing dominoes in the yard with some shipmates and drinking rum *mojitos* until dark.

I said, "He never lived with us."

"Do you understand what he did?" She frowned. "He left us, *mi amor.* Adrift. *Comprendes?*"

I didn't understand Mamá. Each time El Gambao came home she cleaned and cooked and took us for ice cream. But soon Mamá's fish-lipped pouting turned to door-slamming and dish-breaking, and El Gambao would pack his toothbrush and white uniform and leave until the next shipping season.

We last saw him that winter when he waved to us from a Russian tanker named *La Donya.* Before the ship sailed he and Mamá smooched on deck. Emanuel and I sneaked past them, down to the deserted bunk rooms to jump on mattresses. In a drawer I found an empty rum bottle and a statuette of a lady dressed in blue that Mamá later said was Yemayá, goddess of the sea.

"Listen to me," Mamá commanded now. She rubbed Emanuel's skull with kerosene and water to kill the lice. "This country is just a backwater plaintain grove. Now and forever." She wiped her hands on her apron until she left a dark circle. "Tanya, *mija,* our life is about to start."

Mamá always wanted to start life just as I wanted to start a new notebook at school, with neat and crisp lines, waiting to be filled with important dates and bright colors.

She touched my arm and whispered, "Cousin Romy is coming for us. Tomorrow or the next day we could wake up in Cayo Hueso, or *Me-a-me.*" Mamá whispered *Me-a-me* the same way Emanuel and I ate ripe bananas—with greedy, sticky pleasure.

3

IN LAURITA SUAREZ'S KITCHEN, lit by candles—blackouts started at sundown—Mamá promised to pick up Fyor in three days when we returned from "our trip to Havana." I raised my eyebrows at Laurita, a signal for help. But Laurita didn't notice. It was dark and our shadows had disappeared from the walls.

"What's it to you?" Mamá teased Laurita when she asked what we planned to do in Havana.

Laurita smiled. The two were friends from their days before the Revolution at Edison Business Institute, a school run by yankee nuns from Atlanta. They'd studied to become "bilingual secretaries." Mamá quit after she decided she was a person of "letters, not shorthand," and took up with El Gambao, who was then, Mamá claimed, writing poetry. Laurita flunked her Spanish typing tests. She never graduated.

"*Oye,* Lauri," Mamá would say, "explain it to me again. How was it you could type in English but not in Spanish?" They'd laugh in Laurita's kitchen, make fun of the old teachers and sip beer.

But tonight Laurita said, "Look, your problem is"—she paused—"you like to fart higher than your ass, *chica*." She said she did not want to talk about Edison again. "Walls have ears, you know."

Mamá put down her sweaty bottle and stared hard at her friend. "*Que pasa,* Lauri? You worried some snitch down the block will call you a yankee lover?"

"I wonder," Laurita said quietly, "when it will enter your head that it's not a crime to care what people think." She placed her palms on the table, then leaned forward. "Have some respect, Mirella. It's a new chapter now, a new verse. There have to be rules in this country. For once." She looked straight into Mamá's face. "This is what you fought for in the mountains, no?"

Mamá stood. I waved goodbye to Fyor as Mamá pushed me and Emanuel out onto the dark street.

She stopped and pointed to the storefront that housed the block's Committee for the Defense of the Revolution, the CDR. "I never fought for *this.*"

The moon slid behind clouds and Mamá marched down the street, Emanuel and I running to catch up. On the next block she slowed down and recited an interminable poem by a Frenchman. The words buzzed like a mosquito circling my head.

But Laurita was right. Mamá didn't care what anyone thought. She always ran away—last time the mountains, now the open sea.

I wanted to tell her *el Norte* wasn't for us. We weren't yankees. We weren't rich *gusanos* getting back our country club. I wanted to tell her what everyone knew: she was no Storm Captain like she was no *guerrillera.*

Mamá sighed. "Tanya, the world as I know it . . . the world as I know it floats away like a giant bubble." She had the air of one who suffers, is misunderstood.

We passed the corner by the *ceiba* tree. My mouth was dry and sour. I said, "I'm not leaving."

Emanuel threw a pebble. It landed between my feet.

"It doesn't surprise me," Mamá said without looking at me, "that you agree with Laurita."

"I'm not going."

Mamá turned and climbed the porch steps with Emanuel.

Night sounds—the nearby crickets and a faint, faraway cat fight—grew louder. My stomach shut like a fist. Mamá was running again, and this time she'd drag us with her in a flimsy boat across the black water. Finally the thing I'd feared had come. I hated Mamá harder than the Storm Captain hated enemy pirates from the North.

The kerosene lamp inside our house faded, and I ran for the front door, which Mamá had left for me, wide open.

4

AT MIDNIGHT we set out down our pebbled street. The CDR patrol was still making its rounds up the road. We walked fast by the last houses, then by the tin-roofed shacks, candles flickering inside the windows.

Mamá veered toward the bushes with Emanuel. I followed, my gold bracelet sagging cold and heavy inside my panties where Mamá had hidden it. We headed to the harbor where the ferry stopped for Havana-bound passengers. The weeds brushed my chest and I tried to push them from my path the way Storm Captain soldiers bent paper leaves on TV. Mamá pulled Emanuel, and half asleep, he whimpered.

She held the flashlight high. The bushes were taller now, above our heads. The breeze smelled rancid from the oily harbor.

I took Emanuel's hand and pulled him back. "Mamá," I said. "Mamá, let's go home now." But she turned and looked out to the dark. I tried to see what she saw. I tried to imagine what could make someone run away like this, what could be waiting on the other side.

We stepped from the bushes and climbed down to the

rocks. There, in the vast black water, Havana's faraway lights wiggling in the distance, I saw what we were up against. This was no burro ride around familiar hills. Here were the waves that made and kept us an island. With my teeth I pulled the callus on my thumb until I tasted blood.

I closed my eyes and prayed to Yemayá, blue goddess of the sea, that no boat, no raft would come for us this night or any other, that we'd go home and sleep and wake miles from all oceans.

I made a promise, as it was done with the saints. I promised Yemayá that if she let us go now, I would let someone go from me too. "Yemayá," I said in my mind, "if Mamá has to run away to start life, don't let her drag us with her. Let her go alone on a burro as before." I crossed myself the way Abuelita had shown me.

Abuelita said once that something necessary was neither sad nor happy. She said to survive one must make "heart out of tripe." But for me it was the other way around. Heart was what got thrown away.

Mamá turned off the flashlight. We sat on a rock and waited.

Just before daybreak I woke to the sound of water and the rotten smell of the harbor. The sea was calm, stone gray like the sky. There was no *La Quintana,* no cousin Romy.

Dirt and dew had flattened Mamá's hair against her skull. She stooped when she carried Emanuel. "Take the bag," she said.

We turned the corner by the *ceiba* tree, and I saw men in olive green fatigues smoking on our porch. Mamá stopped. The men stood and threw away their cigarettes.

5

One of the compañeros took Mamá by the wrist and said she would have to accompany them to headquarters.

In the parked jeep, Mamá stared ahead and brushed the hair out of her face as if she were trying to empty her mind of thought. She turned once, looked at Emanuel, then at me. She was almost beautiful in the early light.

Laurita came running in her boots and olive green uniform. Mamá said to me, "You're in charge now."

I had thrown Mamá overboard as if she were a pirate from *el Norte*. I had made my pact with Yemayá. Mamá touched my cheek to say goodbye and it hurt all the way inside my mouth as if she had gone in and pulled a tooth as a souvenir. Laurita grabbed our bag and pushed us toward her house, away from the circle of faces watching Mamá in the jeep.

In Laurita's kitchen, Emanuel and I stood against the wall, arms touching. She shut the window and told us to sit. The clock above the stove ticked, loud. Emanuel cried. I ran to the door and my brother followed, but Laurita stepped in front of us and blocked our way.

"Where are they taking her?" I asked.

"The island," was all Laurita said.

She meant Isle of Pines, where the new prison had been built. I didn't tell this to Emanuel, who pulled at my hand. But I remembered Mamá's joke — the Revolution made all things bigger: bigger schools, bigger hospitals. Bigger jails.

Laurita squatted down to Emanuel. "No, *bobito,* no more crying. You're going to the city. Don't you want to see the city?" She pushed his curls away from his eyes.

"From there we can take the train to Abuelita's," I said to him.

"It's too far to the east mountains," Laurita said to me. "Emanuel's little and there's no one to take you."

The clock ticked loudly. "We'll stay here," I said. "I can cook. We'll be no trouble."

Laurita tried to smile, her lips tight across her mouth.

By noon she'd put us on the ferry to Havana. The boat sliced the water and the waves parted and turned to foam. Emanuel screamed about his Storm Captain sword, which someone had taken away at the docks. He tugged at my arm with one hand and pinched his thigh with the other. He was trying not to cry.

At the port a compañero named Rios, arms around us, led us to another jeep. He spoke with a deep lulling voice like a radio announcer's — "Have a seat, children, be comfortable" — then shifted his holster and jumped in next to the driver. We took off down narrow cobbled streets full of potholes. Emanuel and I held our heads down against the wind as if entering a game of jump-rope, our eyes half closed and shoulders cringed up to escape the coming lash of the rope.

The jeep stopped on a street of dark stoops and peeling row houses. Compañero Rios knocked on a faded red door and called out in his mellow voice, "Compañera Petra, compañera, please."

No one answered. He knocked again, this time with the butt of his revolver and looked in through the peephole. He tried to force the knob. Neighbors came to their doors to watch.

"Where do we catch the train to Cáceres?" I asked the driver, though I knew this was no train station.

He shrugged. "These are the orders, *niña*."

A woman with hair cropped like a boy's opened the red door a crack. Compañero Rios said something to her and she screamed "*Alejalo, Saint Alejo*" and shook her hand outward. Behind her a thin old lady watched us. The compañero turned to her and the old lady stared back, hard white hairs sticking out of her bun. She suddenly ran down the steps, holding out her arms to my brother, her face open and grateful.

Compañero Rios followed and said, "Thank you, Compañera Petra, for stepping forward in this front of the struggle."

The old lady held Emanuel's face up in the afternoon glare and her arms dropped in disappointment. She had never seen him before.

The driver helped us out of the jeep and Rios left our bag on the sidewalk. The old lady stared at the idling car and muttered, "No evil lasts a hundred years, nor the body to resist it." Behind us the short-haired woman repeated

"*Alejalo, Saint Alejo*" and her wish was granted: the jeep went away in a cloud of fumes.

That night the old lady said her name only once—Petra Rosa Canuta de Casals. She said she was El Gambao's great-aunt. I remembered an old piano teacher aunt El Gambao had called Melena on account of her big frizzy mane. Mamá had repeated a story how, years ago, she and El Gambao had gone to Melena's Old Havana house with sheet music and demanded that the old lady teach them jazz tunes. But Melena had opened her thick books of scales instead. El Gambao laughed at her. She called him a bum and kicked them both out of her house.

Why the old lady hadn't done the same to Emanuel and me now, I didn't know. Maybe she was getting ready to.

She made us eat runny fried eggs, then sat us in the parlor while she played the piano. When she finished, she led us down the hall to a room with a huge bed and a headboard of swans and fat angels. She handed me a pair of large drawstring pajamas that smelled of old age and closed drawers. Then she left with Emanuel.

I followed. Emanuel and I had never slept apart before.

At her bedroom door, the old lady turned. "Let him be," she whispered. "He's tired. He's had enough trouble for one day." In the room a dark bed sprawled beside a cot, a stuffed duck leaning against the cot's pillow. She shut the door.

I knocked twice, tried the knob. Inside Emanuel cried, then was quiet, and I made my way back, sliding my hands along the wall.

*

In the morning I woke to church bells and a rotten-egg smell in the room. It made me think of the harbor the day before, the ferry chopping up the black, oily bay water. My stomach seesawed again.

I made my way into the sunlit hall, where parakeets threw themselves in a frenzy against their cages. A myna bird shouted "Good morning, good morning, good morning."

In the high-ceilinged parlor old Melena, wiry hair sticking out of her bun, played the same notes back and forth over the yellow keys. Emanuel watched her from the gray sofa, his face scrubbed shiny and curls combed out flat against his head. He wore a sailor jumpsuit stained yellow at the collar, as old as Melena herself. It made him look vaguely like the boy whose giant picture presided over the room from the wall, only the picture had been colorized and the boy's cheeks were too pink, his eyes an unnatural blue.

Emanuel's right leg banged against the wood base of the couch until he saw me and stood. Melena stopped her finger drills to look at me head to toe. Her mouth puckered as if she'd swallowed bitter fruit. She was bony, not soft and round like Abuelita Carmen. She seemed an oversize child but hunched forward as if she had spent her life looking at the ground. "Children, today is Palm Sunday. The bells have rung twice." She paused. "Get ready for mass."

Emanuel and I moved closer to each other. Neither of us knew what mass was. Melena pushed me to the bathroom. Behind gray curtains was a deep, built-in tub like Laurita's. I complained, but Melena's hands were busy opening faucets, testing the water, gathering towels and soap and shampoo bottles. She moved fast, like her parakeets. She wanted me in the tub. She scrubbed my chest, kneecaps, the back of my legs, then a rush of water opened from the ceiling.

The water came down so hard it made me squint, made me want to call out for Mamá to see me. I cried, slowly at first, then I gasped for air, snot running down my lips and chin.

"*Vamos*," Melena said softly. "In church we'll pray to Our Lord for your mother and father."

I wanted nothing to do with saints or prayers ever again.

Melena dressed me in some wrinkled clothes Nelita, the Saint Alejo woman, found in our bag. The skirt was wide and hung past my knees. It belonged to Mamá. Melena pinned a doily from the piano on my wet hair as a veil. She said, "Today marks the triumphal entry of Our Lord *Señor* on the back of a burro to the streets of Jerusalem. So we too will enter the kingdom of heaven." I turned away. That this *señor* rode back to a city on a burro like Mamá did not impress me.

At the end of the mass the priest in purple robe handed out magic palm leaves. I threw mine into the gutter. It twirled, bright green in the filth gushing from the burst sewer pipes. Then it bobbed away. Whether Mamá returned again on a burro or not, triumphant or not, was not a wish I could make true.

One thing was clear: Mamá's wish had been granted. Life was really about to start.

6

THE FIRST of the afternoon pupils made her way to the *pianito* opened like a briefcase on the corner table. She was sent there as punishment, to practice scales without the pleasure of sound.

The roomful of girls sat back as the old lady tossed her knuckle-rapping stick back and forth in her hands. "One learns in this life," she said, "to appreciate things by absence more than by presence."

The dark-skinned girl at the *pianito* was Paula Trenton. I had seen her across Melena's street that first day, gawking at us with the rest of the neighbors. She hit the silent *pianito* keys now with eyes closed. Her silver bracelets chingled. "I play what's in my head," she whispered to me from her bench. I stood in the doorway eating *platanitos* Abuelita Carmen had sent from Cáceres.

Later Paula played her lesson to Melena's inevitable disappointment. I waited. I had saved Paula a *platanito*. "Come to my house," she said.

She lived in a ground-floor apartment across the street,

in a building Melena still called La Santa Maria del Refugio, though the name had been changed to Osvaldo Moya after the revolutionary martyr. The Moya wrapped itself like a horseshoe around a brick courtyard crowded with clotheslines and half-rusted tanks of rainwater for the toilets. The building was flamingo orange, and gray in patches where the paint had faded in the sun.

Paula's apartment was two rooms and a tiny kitchen and bathroom. No one was there. In the bedroom the sun came through the slats and made long rectangles on the bedspread. The big bed was for Paula's mother and stepfather. Paula said she slept on a foldout cot in the living room.

It was then I saw Yemayá again.

Her statue, now dressed in bright yellow, peered down on the room from a high shelf. She was surrounded by candles, a few shells and a bottle of honey.

I stepped out to the terrace. Paula came after me.

"Me and my mother, we're daughters of Ochún." Dark yellow beads peeped out from under the collar of her school uniform. "My mother sees auras."

I shook my head. I didn't want to know.

Her stepfather, she said, was a *santeria* priest, a *babalawo*. "He's the son of Changó, lord of lightning." Paula pointed back inside the room to a smaller saint with a golden sword. "Where is your mother?"

"Sick. She's sick in a hospital," I lied. I knew Mamá was nowhere that comfortable, and my wish to Yemayá had probably put her there.

"My mother can make an offering—"

"It's been done," I interrupted.

Paula squeezed her mouth in sympathy. "Sometimes the saints are forgetful."

I could see Paula had decided to take me under her wing and I didn't resist.

Paula was a year older and shaved her underarms. "You'll feel so fresh," she said in the tiny bathroom, grabbing her mother's razor. "You'll feel the wind in your armpits."

The facial was worse than the shaving. Paula squeezed my skin bit by bit and took out pasty noodles she called "black heads." She showed me each one and had me smell it. I half turned to keep myself from gagging, but I stayed put till the end. After this we saw we could count on each other.

When she was done my face was covered with red dots and bruises. To hide it from nosy neighbors Paula tied a kerchief over my mouth and nose "like an Arab princess."

Melena answered her door and Paula ran off waving goodbye.

"What's with the kerchief? You look like a heathen." Melena pulled the cloth from my face and looked at the ceiling. "At my age, *Señor*, you know I don't need this."

Emanuel sat at the piano, playing the Czerny exercises the old lady had him practice for hours. She'd offered to teach me too — probably out of politeness — but I said no. Melena had chosen my brother as the musical genius, and I didn't love music enough to try to prove her wrong.

She filled the tea kettle in the kitchen. "There are reformatories, places that would take you in a second."

"The Revolution doesn't have reformatories," I said. We had been told this at my new school.

"Like hell they don't."

My face stung. "My brother is bored. He wants to play outside with kids his age."

"And who gave you a candle in this funeral?" Melena asked. She squeezed a chamomile compress to my bruised neck.

There was truth to what she said. She was burying my brother and bringing forth her own dead boy, the one in the picture.

"He's my brother," I said. "He's not your son."

Emanuel stopped playing and Valentin the myna bird started his "Good night let's all sleep in a hurry" song. Nelita's bedroom door banged shut.

Melena did not blink.

"Unfortunately for you," she smiled, "I'm not as crazy as you think."

I closed my eyes and let her plaster compresses over my face. I was almost glad, in a perverse way, that for now this was home.

7

EVERY DAY THAT WEEK we went to mass. It was Holy Week, Melena said. It was Lent, and we had to expiate our sins.

The same *Señor* who had come triumphant that Sunday was dead by Friday. It was sad how even then people's intentions got twisted and their worst wishes came to pass. I smiled once, when a man was said to have shouted at the cross, "If you're the son of God why don't you save yourself?" It made sense to me.

In his sermon Padre Llerena hissed, his teeth the color of milk custard. We were all "men of little faith," he shouted. We were not worthy. He seemed insulted. Melena snoozed beside me. She roused when the choir stopped singing and afterward she pushed her way down the communion line. Emanuel played piano on his lap, fingers trotting over invisible keys, back and forth across his thighs. From their niches, saints looked to us with painted glass eyes as if there was something we could do about their misery.

The next day I brought Paula along to keep me company, and Melena seemed pleased. She quoted Matthew: "And He will make you fishers of men."

After mass people milled around the entrance. We quietly filled Paula's plastic purse with holy water to take back to her mother for *santeria* jobs. Melena pretended not to notice. Later she told me a rambling story about Don Melvino Trenton, Paula's grandfather. "Chinese mulatto from Jamaica. Calm and polite, hard-working," she said. "He went out every morning dressed in a hat and starched pantaloons until the day he died. His wife passed for white. Unfortunately her folks came from the country and she loved voodoo. From what I hear she passed it on to Paula's mother. Listen to me." Melena paused. "I want you to tell me what goes on in that house. And don't you eat or drink anything there. Ever."

I understood Paula's mother's saints better than I did Melena's thorny-headed statues. With the saints you didn't humiliate yourself listing sins and you didn't bow down as if they were royalty. You danced and cooked for them if you wanted their favor, and if they didn't deliver, you threatened to put them on bread and water, as Paula's mother did. And you didn't repeat prayers every night before sleeping to avoid hell after this life. As far as Melena knew, nobody was sure they were going to heaven. You assumed, she said, you'd at least end up in purgatory if you didn't kill anybody. But with the saints you set your own terms and the results were verifiable.

Melena put me in Sunday school, and for a while Paula came along too. Our catechism teacher, Señorita Eugenia, studied at the university. She was in her late twenties, had severe acne and very small breasts. Her skirts were short as if to compensate for her lack of beauty. She sneezed from allergies all morning long.

She gave us each a pamphlet with a one-word title — "Adolescence" — and from behind her tissues, she explained that adolescence was a time of confusion and danger. Paula rearranged her silver bracelets. "Your bodies are changing," Señorita Eugenia continued, "but you need to wait before you act upon those changes. Hormones determine" — she was a biology major — "the development of breasts, the onset of menses, the growth of pubic hair and interest in the opposite sex. Once menses ensue, one must be very careful because one can now be impregnated." She paused to sneeze and clear her throat. "The Church urges us to fight base desires. Any boy who pushes us to sin is not worthy."

After class Paula and I walked ahead of Melena and Emanuel down the open porticos and narrow sidewalks of the old part of the city. Men sat on stoops, smoking and talking. Whenever we walked by they stopped their chatter and stared. We looked straight ahead.

Two men broke away from their group. They leaned close to us and whispered "sweet thing" and "*belleza*," mostly to Paula, who already had breasts and pubic hair and menses.

I wondered whether men all over the world stood on streets waiting to impregnate women. If so, I didn't understand what was so great about impregnating others that they dedicated so much of their time to it. I wondered why sometimes men hid behind columns and showed their things to girls walking by.

It happened to us once on our walk home from church, so fast I didn't see the thing, only the open flap of his pants and the man who'd whistled at us, his face hard but pleading like one of Melena's statues. Paula nudged me to keep walking. "Never look. Anybody worth talking to knows your name."

Later I asked Paula about these men, but she saw no cause for alarm. "They only do it for entertainment," she said. "Some boys pick their noses, others whisper dirty words or pull out their things."

Now at the Moya courtyard, Paula's mother sat with rollers in her hair and painted her toenails. She kissed the bangs on Paula's forehead, then glanced at our pamphlets. Paula asked if men too had hormones.

"Listen, *niñas*," Paula's mother said, "A man is by nature a louse. A man wants to stick his *pipi* where it doesn't belong. All the time. A man has no judgment of things beyond desire or vanity. A woman keeps a cool head and stays out of dark alleys, that's all."

None of this sounded appealing. Then Paula asked about love. Paula's mother pulled out the cotton balls she had wedged between her toes.

"This is where a woman's hormones come in. Men bring a lot of pleasure to life. You'll see, *niñas*" — she paused and smiled — "if you're lucky."

8

THERE WAS NO WORD from Mamá all summer.

Then fall came, the hot air lost its dampness and a letter arrived in the mailbox, the first one in months. It was addressed to me, to Señorita Tanya del Carmen Casals Villalta. But the writing wasn't Mamá's.

The letter was typed on official stationery from the Ministry of the Interior. I read it to myself a few times, then out loud to Melena and Emanuel.

Querida Tanya

I am happy to report that your mother has completed her rehabilitation program and vocational training at Model Facility Patricio Lumumba. For her probationary period of three months she will stay with me and have regular visits with you. I will be in touch with a specific date you can expect her.

My love to Emanuel, regards to Compañera Petra, and you receive my most sincere affection.

In revolutionary solidarity,
Laurita Suarez Mendoza
Administrative Assistant

P.S. Fyor is well, still hunting down rabbits. I feed him and he sleeps in your yard, under the lime tree.

After our first night in the city Emanuel never cried for Mamá again because Melena told him he had to be her "little man," but the letter was too much and he peed in his pants and all over one of Melena's antique rugs from the Orient. Melena changed his clothes and whispered things in his ear but I saw everything had changed. Now Mamá was coming home and Emanuel could refuse Melena's stained piano books and her yellowed shirts. I could see holes everywhere in the net she'd cast around him.

The old lady must have known it too because that afternoon she picked up her bag and went out. She even forgot to make Emanuel practice his Czerny.

Emanuel and I stayed outside while she was gone. Nelita yelled for us to come in but we sat on the stoop. The nightly cannon blast marked nine o'clock and we took our turns at hopscotch by Melena's peeling door, first with Paula and later with an older, scruffier crowd of children whose parents did not seem to care enough to call them home to bed.

The night breeze scattered the evening cooking odors and the moldy stench of crumbling buildings. Moonlight fell on the housefronts, their cracks and chipping walls pocked and shadowy.

That night Emanuel and I felt lucky. Mamá was coming. We were going home.

Close to midnight Melena came back, her crazy hair more disheveled than usual, her dress dusty and her pantyhose wrinkled at the calves. She didn't seem angry at finding us alone on the curb, Emanuel asleep, his head on my lap.

Instead she said, "*Bien.* Your mother is coming to live with us on the fifteenth."

I felt as if something inside me had crumbled.

Emanuel jumped up and hugged Melena's legs. She smiled briefly, then looked me in the face. "You say nothing?"

"Live here?" I asked.

"With all of us." The old lady smiled.

"How did you do it?" I asked, though I really wanted to ask how, in a preemptive strike of her own, she could swallow my family whole.

"I have old students in high places," Melena said. She dropped her purse and sat on the stoop, Emanuel by her knees like a lapdog. She stroked his soft curly hair.

9

AT MIDMORNING we stepped from our bus into the entrance of the Aeropuerto Internacional. "We're late." Melena frowned. Uniformed women dragged suitcases down a long hallway, and groups of red-faced Russians spoke loudly, as if they owned the place.

After a sharp turn, Melena pointed to a glassed-in room she called the fishbowl. Waiting inside was Mamá. She was leaning forward in her seat, her hair cut short. She sagged, as if she needed to be pumped full of air. Her hands were bony and she cracked her knuckles.

Emanuel threw himself against the glass and stayed there, glued like a starfish. Mamá looked up and thrust her hand to Emanuel's from her side of the glass.

I pressed my face to the glass too. My legs loosened. Everything turned dim and slow, then went black.

When I woke up I smelled alcohol and my panties stuck to my behind. Mamá was massaging my forehead. "Little Tanya, *mi frijolito.*" She hadn't called me that in years. "I see you missed me." She smiled vaguely. "I missed you too." Her eyes were dark and wet and there was no restless mischief in them anymore.

10

At first Melena cooked Mamá lunches of *arroz con pollo* and *yuca* bought at steep prices from the neighborhood black marketeers. "The devil take the ration books," Melena said. "Mirella, you have to recover." The old lady served heaping portions but Mamá slyly dumped hers on my plate. I ate. I ate to keep things flowing, to prolong harmony. I ate because I was too nervous to stop.

Bad signs were there—portents, Paula called them. Mamá was up nights sitting by the window, cigarette lit. She was silent when Melena spoke of the future. "You have to think of the children. If we all pitch in they can grow up nicely, not like hoodlums." The old lady talked at night while she washed cups and saucers. I listened from the parlor. Mamá leaned against the kitchen wall, staring at her cigarette. She let the old woman go on. "It's not too late, even for the girl. She's bright enough, though bristly. Manuelito is musical, like my Ronaldo, may he rest in peace. A marvelous sensitivity. I can get him into the conservatory when he turns ten."

Other times at breakfast Melena asked sneaky questions. "What did they feed you there . . . in that place?"

Mamá had not spoken about "that place" since her return. "Breakfast," she said, "was milk and stale bread. Breakfast was better than lunch." She looked away, putting an end to the old lady's questions.

Emanuel had to touch Mamá's skin—her hand, neck, knee—at all times. He did not go outside unless Mamá held him against her side. During meals he sat on her lap and refused to feed himself. When Mamá first returned, Melena did not insist he practice piano. But after a while she tried to encourage him. "Show your mamá how well you play." He looked to Mamá for reassurance but her dreamy, lost air made him more fearful. He held on to Mamá's neck and yelled back, "I don't play anything."

The old lady turned away stiff and iron-willed, but without reproach. It looked as if she had given up control. She'd even stopped yelling at lazy pupils.

On Mamá's second week back Laurita Suarez came to visit on a brand-new motorcycle. She had tied Fyor down in the sidecar and when they stopped at the curb I saw that his eyes were bloodshot. He shook uncontrollably. I kissed him, put a blanket over him. For a few minutes he didn't seem to know who I was.

Laurita gossiped with Mamá about the old Regla neighborhood, and the beer she brought loosened Mamá's tongue. I sprawled on the floor next to Fyor and rubbed his belly. Mamá and Laurita sat close together on the couch like schoolgirls and at one point Mamá cried a little. She was still skinny from her months at Isle of Pines.

"You can start over," Laurita whispered. "You will start over."

Mamá blew her nose and stared, glassy-eyed. Then she sent me to my room.

I heard them leave on Laurita's motorcycle. Later I smelled beer and strange perfumes as Mamá slid next to me in bed.

That afternoon Mamá wore makeup and rollers in her hair. We sat on Melena's stoop. "So who do you know in the neighborhood?" she asked.

I named a few people: the retarded Salmerón twins from the bakery, Alfredo Nilan the Beautiful from Paula's building, Paula Trenton, of course, and her mother, Carina, and stepfather.

"Strange name, Trenton."

"From Jamaica. My best friend here."

Mamá had a way of listening that made me feel grown up, smart.

"Paula invited me to a mass at her house tonight." I wasn't as much asking permission as sharing a secret. Mamá looked at me intently. "Melena won't let me go. She doesn't like Paula's mother and her voodoo religion."

Mamá held down her short skirt as she stood. "Please ask your friends"—she smiled—"if it's all right for your mother to come too."

That night Melena was in a brooding mood until Mamá said Emanuel would stay behind. He cried and kicked the table leg. Mamá's beer glass fell and smashed against the dark tiles. Melena took him to the parlor and soon after, we heard a fiery rendition of Czerny and Melena praising him loudly.

Before we left, Mamá took me to our bedroom and sprayed me with Florida water she kept in a perfume bottle as "protection," she said, "against evil eyes. It's not that I believe in this stuff"—she dabbed beneath my ear—"but I respect it." Then, "Perfect skin. Like your father's." I closed my eyes. Her fingers were cool against my hot cheeks.

Paula's apartment smelled "like a funeral," Mamá whispered after we entered. The heavy scent of jasmine made me sneeze. Paula's mother led us to a line of women waiting to wash with the holy water Paula and I had stolen little by little from Melena's church. Mamá and I wet our hands and foreheads and the backs of our necks. Petals floating in the basin stuck to Mamá's arms.

At the front of the room sat a man younger than Mamá. His chest was sunken and small like a girl's. He seemed fragile, as if he could be toppled by a gust of wind. Paula's stepfather, who could touch ceilings with his fingertips, leaned forward to whisper to the little man and covered him from view. I thought he might gobble him up and spit out the bones like a storybook giant.

Two, then three men beat on drums and the women sang and swayed. They sprang from their chairs and swiveled their hips and swung their arms. The little man whispered, eyes closed, then suddenly he joined them and lifted his arms and the whole room filled with shouts. His arms still raised, he began turning fast, swirling out of control until he bumped into the holy water basin and the water splattered over the first row of guests. Then he crumpled to the floor.

Everyone was silent when Paula's stepfather lifted the limp body and sat him in a chair. The little man's head hung back. Then he hunched forward as though he were very old, and began speaking the broken Spanish that African slaves used on TV.

"Greeting," he said, "from Francisco Siete Rayo."

People leaned toward his voice. They spoke to him as if they'd known him for years. "Old man," said Paula's stepfather, "tell me and my wife about our *ilé.*" He meant his *santeria* home, his religious family.

The little man leaned back in his seat and lit a cigar. "Tree about to give fruit," he said in his TV Spanish. "White people knock on your door. You say all right. White women. You say all right. But not in your heart." He pummeled his chest with his fist. Paula's mother sat back. "Your heart stay shut to them. Your heart not for sale. Understand Francisco Siete Rayo." Paula's stepfather nodded. "You keep your pant on. Trouble ahead but you ride and wait. Trouble bring you business and pleasure and sweet fruit. Enjoy. Keep heart hidden."

Paula's mother said, "I want to ask about my brother, Carlito."

"Speak loud. Old man can't hear."

"*Carlito.* Nobody's heard from him for months."

"Bad business. Must spill goat blood to quench thirst of saint. A beautiful young *mulato* like Carlito, *salsoso,* delicious. Ochún fall in love with him. Must distract Ochún away." A woman put her hand on Carina's shoulder in sympathy.

Others asked about health, love, family, political connections, money. Only Mamá and I were left.

"New white girl here." The little man pointed to us in the back. People turned in their seats.

"Mirella and her daughter, Tanya," Paula's mother said. We stood and walked to the front.

"White girl," the man said to Mamá. "Oh, white girl. You bring lot of grief here." He rested against the back of his chair. "Somebody betray you. Somebody close. You suffer from this person envy. She betray you." Mamá did not move. "Forget revenge. She come to you, she come to you now, and you give her rope to hang. Take this, white girl." The man blew cigar smoke on a set of red beads, stood up and handed them to Mamá. "Put in finger when you talk to her. You rub the bead and bad woman rot inside and burn like firewood."

I didn't know I'd envied Mamá. I stood next to her holding my sides with wet palms, waiting for Francisco Siete Rayo to tell my secret. Then everyone would know how I'd betrayed my mother out of fear, lack of heart.

The old man laughed. "You"—he pointed to me—"your little head turn thing round and round till you and everybody dizzy but you don't know nothing." He tapped his forehead. "Nothing. Put this"—he turned and handed me a dry gray rose from the table behind him. "Put in water under your bed for seven day. As it bloom so you bloom."

11

THE MOYA COURTYARD was deserted after midnight. Paula and I made pictures by scratching sections of peeling paint from the wall. I worked on a long-tailed dinosaur and Paula carved a woman's profile, big crooked nose and sharp teeth. "Self-portrait," she said. Paula's mother and Mamá smoked black-market cigarettes and drank beer on the Moya steps. Carina leaned toward Mamá. "You know what you need in this world?"

Mamá smiled. Late-night, drunken talk pleased her. "Guts," she answered.

Carina laughed. She and Mamá had become friends in the few weeks since the mass with Francisco Siete Rayo. On Fridays Mamá helped Carina iron her long curly hair and color it mercurochrome red. Some nights we ate at Paula's and went back to Melena's only to sleep.

At first my brother cried at the window. I asked Mamá to include him but she said the grown-up talk would bore him.

I saw then Emanuel was Mamá's price tag for peace

with the old lady. And we needed Melena even more now that rations lasted only two weeks out of the month. Condensed milk was good currency on the black market. Melena was old and received fifteen cans a month, and the cans fed us: three for a loaf of bread, five for two drumsticks, seven for a bar of soap.

On those evenings when we left Emanuel staring from the window, Mamá bragged about his future to Carina. "Old Tia Petra'll make him a pianist," Mamá said one night while she filed Carina's nails.

"She'll make him a fairy," Paula's stepfather said from the doorway. He was home from work, sweaty, smelly, loud.

Carina stood and kissed him on the mouth. He grabbed her rear, keeping his hand there for a moment. Then he spanked once where he'd grabbed, as if she'd misbehaved while he was gone.

"I don't mind fairies," Mamá said in the ironic tone she used with him. "I'm not sure why you would."

He turned to Carina. "Why is this woman in my house pestering me when all I want is to screw my wife and go to sleep."

"*Papi*, the children." Carina put a finger to her lips.

Paula's stepfather took Mamá's beer bottle and gulped it down. He looked straight at Mamá and she didn't turn away. She seemed determined to hold her own.

They had argued before but Mamá had always backed off, let him have the last word. It was his home and I could see she wanted, above all, to be asked back.

His name was Nicolás Dolores Parra, and Paula had

warned me never to use his middle name. It was a woman's name and he was ashamed of it. We secretly called him Loló, even when he was present. We pretended Loló was the name of Paula's stuffed seal and he never caught on. Paula hated him, more, I thought, than was called for. She said he was *un bruto,* selfish and spoiled. I could see it, but her contempt was strong and a little scary.

He brought her gifts that he said were from his job at the warehouse and from *santeria* clients—all for his "daughter." Paula curled her lip. "He thinks he can buy me with some trinket from a girlfriend." Since our move to the city I'd tried not to look surprised about anything, but this time I flinched. "He has girlfriends?"

"You're so young," Paula said in disdain. "You know nothing."

That year Loló's reputation as a *babalawo* had grown. People came on Saturdays and Sundays, all the way from Miramar and Guanabo so he could read their future with cowrie shells. Soon Carina and he had no more room in the tiny apartment for all the people and gifts. In exchange for weekly consultations, Mamá stored the loot for them in Melena's spare room behind the old lady's back.

I worried. To run any kind of business with profits like Loló's was illegal. The CDR could turn us in to state security. But Mamá seemed to think Loló had everything covered. "Nicolás sees Party members. From the Central Committee, understand? They're clients."

She must have been right. Paula's family didn't hide

their good fortune—they went out for pizza, had dresses made, even one for me, with expensive black-market material. The CDR asked no questions. Paula sketched fashions we'd seen on the street and we took her drawings to one of Loló's clients, Yolanda, a wrinkled seamstress in Muralla's old Polish district. Yolanda lived in one room in a crumbling building, with twenty tenants that shared one bathroom. Her room stank of urine from the night's chamber pot. But she knew people who could get her foreign material—the elastic *laster* girls went crazy for and the bright gold-threaded scarves they wrapped around the rollers in their hair.

Paula and I got invited to small, private *fiestas* in the suburbs. Mamá took us to these parties on the bus and later picked us up. Carina made excuses for Paula to Loló, who forbade Paula to date or dance. She'd tell him we'd gone to the movies, to a school play. We wore Carina's eyeliner and shadow—a mix of blue chalk and deodorant paste—and sat on the girls' side of the room watching the couples dance. Several boys asked Paula to dance but she didn't know the new moves and refused to "act mongoloid."

At one of the *fiestas* in a newly confiscated *gusano* mansion, Paula met Leandro. Yellow-haired, gray-eyed, he was too skinny and shy, though he was the host of the party and everybody was his friend. Red patches of acne spread like chicken pox across his white skin.

Paula would not dance but asked him to sit with her out on the long terrace. I watched them through the window. Paula pushed the bangs from her eyes. He looked down at the floor. When the party ended he shook her hand.

On the bus home Mamá wanted to know all about the *fiesta*. "Seemed like a good one," she said. "Must have been the house of a Party leader. This used to be an exclusive yankee neighborhood. You'd hear English spoken in the streets." She paused, then said to Paula, "You know, your Fifteens is coming up. Nicolás has enough *plata* to rent the 1800 Restaurant and a live band. Your mother and I will work on him—"

"I don't want some ridiculous party for my stepfather's glory." Paula's tone had such bitter authority I was proud to know her. Mamá was silent the rest of the way.

Back at Melena's Mamá said, "That girl's a mule."

"So?" I answered.

"So don't you talk back to me," Mamá said. "You two are splinters from the same stick."

I smiled, though even then I feared it wasn't true.

12

THE NEXT DAY Laurita brought the official word: Mamá was to report to work that Monday at a matchbox factory in East Havana.

The two women faced each other on Melena's gray couch. Nelita served lemonade. Mamá read the letter out loud, pausing between words as if she had trouble understanding what they said. Then she left the room.

Laurita looked past me to the dusty curtains where Mamá had disappeared into the hallway. She asked me about Fyor. "He's getting old," I said. "He's not how he used to be."

"Happens to all of us," she said, and folded and refolded the empty envelope. A thin layer of sweat appeared above her upper lip.

Mamá returned, her right hand in one of her dress pockets. She fiddled with something inside. "As you well know, *mi amiga,*" Mamá said, her voice brittle with anger, "this job is for the senile or the criminally insane, neither of which I am yet."

"I'm sorry, Mirella. I really am." Laurita looked up at Mamá. "I told my boss you were a fighter in the mountains, one of us. I explained about El Gambao, how he defected and you thought you'd follow him. Because of the children, I told him. You realize your mistake now. He said all available office jobs are top security. He said once you are fully integrated into the system—"

"But I *am* integrated, Lauri," Mamá said in a low, sarcastic tone. "You all integrated me, remember? All those slogans in my ears, the slaps, the hunger. You integrated me until there was nothing left to integrate."

"Mirella, *perdoname,* who is 'you all'?"

Mamá moved her right hand furiously in her pocket. "When I was there, in that place you all call a rehabilitation center, I thought about you constantly. That night you said it wasn't a crime to care what people thought. You were right. I should have paid more attention to what *you* were thinking." Mamá paused. Laurita rubbed her lower belly with both hands. "I'm sure somebody tipped you off about me. And if somebody tipped you off, then you *had* to turn me in."

"Nobody tipped me off, Mirella. Nobody had to. You're a fool." Laurita stood up. "What did you expect? You always do whatever shit you please and now it's caught up with you. It's still catching up with you."

"I understand you had to turn me in," Mamá said. "Even profit from it. What I don't understand is why you enjoy it so."

Laurita doubled over and lurched toward the door. Mamá stood still, took her hand out of her pocket.

Days later we heard through the Regla grapevine that Laurita'd had emergency surgery for a ruptured appendix. When the news came Mamá locked herself in the bathroom and stayed there so long Emanuel and I took turns peeing in the hedge behind Melena's house. Mamá came out in late afternoon. She smelled of vomit and so did the bathroom. "Hide these from me." She handed me Francisco Siete Rayo's magic beads. "No matter how much I beg, never tell me where they are."

Francisco Siete Rayo's beads had pierced Laurita's gut and burned her insides. She was the traitor he'd warned Mamá about, not me.

But what scared Mamá was the power of her own vindictiveness. I knew something of this — how bad thoughts brewed inside till one day they sifted upward like smoke and changed the color of the air. The powers outside simply waited to help them, and you, along.

13

MAMÁ CAME HOME from the matchbox factory each evening with an aching back and swollen feet. She had put me in charge of getting her footbath ready so when she stepped through the door she could throw down her purse and sprawl across Melena's old couch, dunk her feet in the warm water, prop a pillow behind her waist. Then she drank her first beer, took three aspirin and sat alone in the half light, eyes closed, right hand propping her forehead.

She wouldn't sit still long. By seven o'clock we would knock on Carina's door so Mamá could have her private *consulta* with Loló if he was free. But the more Mamá consulted Loló, the less Carina treated us like friends. She no longer fed us, and she made us wait outside like the rest of Loló's clients.

One night, a few weeks after Paula and I buried Francisco Siete Rayo's beads in a planter, the two of us waited outside for Mamá to come from her session with Loló. Paula and I looked inside the lit apartment through the front window. Mamá had gone in hours before and now she sat slumped in a corner of the sofa while Loló played the drums. Carina danced; she pushed out her behind and moved her hips in a circle. Her shoulders shook. She teased Loló by sitting on his lap and then escaping his giant's hands.

"Hey you," Loló yelled at Mamá. "You dance too."

"White people can't dance," Carina said, laughing. Loló was white but laughed with her.

"*Oye.*" Loló walked over to Mamá, grabbed her under the arm and pulled her to her feet. He spun her around but she collapsed, her chin plopping to her chest. He and Carina sat Mamá on the sofa and then he slapped Mamá hard on the cheek.

Paula and I ran in. "We're going home," I said.

Loló slapped Mamá again. "She can't go anywhere like this." He raised his hand again above Mamá's face.

I leaned over Mamá, blocking his arm. Carina brought over a wet rag and a bottle of rum. Loló forced the bottle between Mamá's lips. She coughed and spit up. I held her hand.

"The saints are calling you," Loló whispered to her. "They're calling you to be initiated."

"Eat something." Carina brought Mamá a plate of cold yellow rice.

"We're going home now," I said. I suddenly remembered Melena's warning not to eat or drink anything in that house.

"Let them go home," Paula said to Loló.

"*Oye, niña,* children speak when hens pee gold, understand?" Loló said.

"Let them go," Paula yelled. Carina turned from Mamá

and screamed at Paula to shut up. I helped Mamá from the couch and walked her to the door.

Loló grabbed Paula's ponytail and yanked her head back against his chest. With his free hand he played with her long black curls.

I held Mamá by the waist and dragged her through the Moya courtyard. We reached the corner, where a crowd of young men looked up from their dominoes game. One finally stepped forward and slipped his shoulder under Mamá's right arm. Her weight lifted and I straightened a little.

Nelita let us in the house and the young man lowered Mamá onto the sofa. Melena thanked him and almost pushed him out the door.

"What did she have over there?" She unbuttoned the top button of Mamá's blouse, her bony fingers fast and steady. Mamá's eyes were drawn back up as if some great thing were about to drop from the ceiling.

"She went in the room with Loló, then she came out," I said. Melena looked at me. "Paula's stepfather, I mean . . . She went in alone."

"What did he give her?"

I shook my head. "How would I know?"

"The same way you know to bring her here when your little witchcraft games turn scary." She paused. "You do know she's been drugged, don't you?"

I knew nothing. Why would anyone want my mother to pass out, her eyes screwed up to the top of her head? Mamá did almost anything of her own free will, under the right sort of persuasion.

"It's sad. Your mother is a sad case." Melena didn't seem to care how her words stung. "I'm sorry, *niña*. You're too young to see this, but you might as well learn from it."

The two of us carried Mamá into the bathroom and settled her, naked, into a cool bath. Dull bruises were scattered here and there across Mamá's buttocks. Melena saw them too.

"What are these?" I asked.

Melena didn't answer.

"What are these?"

"Listen to me." Melena grabbed my shoulder. "Your mother has been drugged and brainwashed and who knows what else."

I stood still. Mamá was coming to. Her eyes tried to focus. Melena spoke softly to Mamá, the way one speaks to a baby. "Mirella, *mija*, how do you feel?"

For a few hours I thought about what Melena knew and didn't know about Mamá. The old lady sensed some evil in her gut and ran with it. But she *knew* nothing.

"Loló likes to get rough," Paula said the next day on our walk home from school. "He gets that way when he's ready to — you understand?" This time I didn't flinch. And I didn't ask for details. I nodded, as if Paula had read this in a book about circus freaks. Or maybe she'd imagined it when listening to voices, late at night, through the thin walls of her apartment.

But her eyes were glassy and hard, and I knew better.

"I won't stay in that house much longer," she said.

Until then I'd thought of Paula as tall, bitter, invincible. But now I saw she was just my height. She played with a stuffed seal. She laughed at sixth-grade Pepito jokes and when I tickled her, she squealed like Emanuel.

"Where would you go?"

I saw Loló across the street, his eyes on me. Paula veered left and I ran.

At home Melena asked me what was wrong. I wouldn't say. The old lady was lucky to be so old and know so little.

14

THE RETARDED Salmerón twins from the bakery lined up the folding chairs in the parlor, then sat in front row seats, stiff and attentive. It was a piano recital in honor of Melena's eighty-fifth birthday and the martyrdom of Santa Cecilia, patroness of music, at the hands of a pagan judge.

Pupils and parents took their seats. The little girls wore starchy puffed-out skirts and their mothers velvet chokers and long homemade earrings of twisted wire. Nelita had polished the furniture and brushed the cobwebs from the door frames. The piano was tuned and a clear vase of white and yellow daisies sat on top, the water inside vibrating with each student's nervous warmups.

Paula was the only pupil not invited to perform. After Mamá's fainting spell and mysterious bruises, Melena believed Paula to be a member of the "witches' coven" from across the street. I did not contradict her. Melena liked having personal enemies, thought herself worthy of them. "*Niña,* always remember"—she winked and pointed to her right temple—"the devil knows more from being old than from being the devil."

For the concert the old lady wore her Sunday clothes: a cotton mustard gown to her calves and pantyhose. Nelita wrestled down Melena's frizz with old men's hair grease. Without the Beethoven mane, Melena's face was distorted. Her nose stuck out too far and her ears bent from her head like an elephant's.

Emanuel was the star of the concert. Melena had managed to get him a new suit. It sagged from his thin shoulders. But when I saw him sit, the last pupil at the piano, I realized the old lady had given him more than the suit and the lessons. She'd given him a way of seeing himself, of reaching a depth of concentration unknown to me, to anyone in our family.

I thought I'd be sorry to watch the old lady strut her triumph over us. But I felt almost the same peace as before Mamá ran off to fight in the mountains. The black and white keys disappeared beneath Emanuel's hands and he closed his eyes, swayed back and forth, paused, then pressed the keys louder. I stood, moved by the music. Someone sitting behind me pulled at my skirt. Ruth Pendestal, our next door neighbor, pushed her paper fan against my buttocks. She grimaced as if her fan covered something unspeakable.

Mamá stayed in bed during the concert. For the past month she'd taken advantage of her diagnosis of "pernicious anemia" to take a leave from work, shut the drapes in our bedroom, and chain-smoke. The night she'd "fallen ill," as Melena called it, and I'd dragged her home from

Loló's, the doctor came and drew blood with a syringe. After he left Nelita said *santeros* liked to drink human blood. This was why Mamá was anemic.

I'd said, "They fly at night like bats looking for skinny damsels to suck on and this time they picked Mamá." Both women turned to me, stone-faced. Melena finally said, "One of these days something will happen to you that will teach you respect. I just hope it doesn't kill you."

The old lady's words must have come true. Somehow, without my knowledge, I had gone to the bathroom in my panties. The brown mess had seeped into my muslin skirt. Ruth Pendestal had seen it.

I walked into our bedroom, then passed Mamá's side of the bed. Cigarette butts filled her dirty *café* cups. Some days she didn't get up at all and the whole bed was warm from her body and reeked of sweat and smoke.

Mamá reached out for me.

"I soiled my pants," I mumbled. "It was an accident."

She pulled me to her and smelled the spot. "This is not what you think," she said. "Does your stomach hurt?"

I shook my head.

"It will soon enough."

She leaned back and blew out a puff of smoke, then pointed to her dresser. "Pull a rag and two safety pins out of the green box. One pin goes in front, one in back. Make sure the bulge doesn't show. Don't wear white to school all week." She smiled vaguely. "Welcome to womanhood." Then she looked away.

I said to the back of her matted hair, "Why can't you come out and see Emanuel play?"

"I'm tired," Mamá said. "Let me be."

When she fell asleep, I looked under the bed for the flower Francisco Siete Rayo had given me. I found it in Melena's pot, where I'd forgotten it months before. If it had ever bloomed, by now it had dissolved into foul-smelling muck.

15

MONDAY MORNING at school, Paula managed to squeeze herself in front of me during formation, though she wasn't in my Pioneer unit. She pulled down the collar of her uniform and I counted—two on the right, one on the left—dark vampire marks that reminded me of Mamá's bruises.

Later, at recess, Paula didn't like my comparison. "*These* feel good."

The hickeys on her neck were proof of her love—at fifteen, she was secretly engaged to Leandro.

We stood by the wall in the school's cemented patio. Boys at the foot of the stairs tried looking up the skirts of girls coming down the steps. When a boy spotted some panties, he called out the color. Other boys patted him on the back.

Paula leaned against the wall. Leandro's father, she said, was the boss of a ministry subdivision in charge of exporting and importing items related to art and culture. Paula told me this word for word, as if she'd read it in a brochure. Leandro's mother shopped at the special store for Party leaders. "Yesterday she bought goat cheese there," Paula said. "Smelled like vomit."

Aside from sucking on Paula's neck, Leandro's habits were not that weird. He was on the school swim team, which made him a member of the Communist Youth. After practice Paula went with him to long meetings, nudged him as he dozed off in the back of crowded rooms.

At these meetings I pictured talk of hidden cameras and tapped phones, like in Scotland Yard movies. Paula pursed her lips when I told her this. "You are so mongoloid. Leandro doesn't even do guard on the block. His father used to work for El Che, you know."

If there was one person above suspicion in the country, it was El Che—sincere, bright, painfully handsome. And dead. The day of the ambush in Bolivia, Mamá swore someone should ask Fidel about it. Even Melena had cursed. "Who in this country of thieves and cowards dares to ask that bastard anything, including who his real father is?"

This had not impressed me. I was automatically on the side of fatherless children.

Paula liked it that Leandro had promised her perfume and scarves from the next batch that "came in"—gifts to Leandro's father from foreigners or, more likely, bribes by locals allowed to travel on official business. They smuggled in everything—jewelry to toothpaste—to trade on the black market but except for Leandro's small favors, Paula gave little thought to rubbing elbows with the country's higher-ups. She had one priority—escape—but we didn't speak of it, not until we'd hatched a plan and set it in motion.

Then our feelings would not matter. There'd be no way to backtrack.

Recess was over. We held our skirts and walked up the stairs.

16

DARKNESS must have come gradually to Melena's eyes.

The world must have edged itself in shadows over her like the daguerreotypes on her mantelpiece: Melena's father holding a cane upright between his legs; her mother, so tightly corseted her bosom puffed up like a pillow.

"It's like a slow sunset," the old lady said about her blindness one morning in the parlor. I had just run in there the way my brother did, stopping suddenly with a skip at the end. Melena, who'd learned to recognize us by our walk, softened her face and spoke in a gentle voice, as if to an old friend. I stayed still for as long as I could stand it. Then I left her alone in the bright room, speaking in her soft tones to no one.

My idea of love was Mamá's way with us. She kissed us, made jokes, took us in on her schemes, yelled at us and finally forgot us. I also knew the love between me and Paula: mutual protection in the face of trouble, like looking at your face in the mirror and loving it only because it is yours.

But the old lady's feeling for my brother was physical like the world. Her love for Emanuel was there, in the house. I bumped against it at the table, where she'd set his special bowl before he woke each morning. I rubbed against it in the fresh towel she left hanging for him in the bathroom. Every day this love gave Emanuel a sense of being worthy because she was there, unmovable, bearing witness. I thought love like that was magic and would never happen to me. Mainly because I wanted it and wanting it upset the magic — like a child carrying a glass of water: someone says "Be careful" and there it goes, spinning to the floor. Melena's pleasure must have come from watching Emanuel set his glass down safely on the table. It must have come from giving to someone who'd only understand later, if at all, what had been given.

Meanwhile, Leandro's pleasure had wandered below Paula's neck. One Saturday in October Paula came to Melena's back gate. I ran to her with Fyor, who licked her ankles. Then Paula and I took a walk down the block, "for security reasons." Paula whispered the story to me in starts and spurts.

The night before, she and Leandro drove by the seawall in his father's Alfa-Romeo, the top down, the breeze rough on Paula's ironed curls. There was something about Leandro's hands, she said, so light she found herself standing still while they roamed up and down, up and down her body. They ended up on the Rampa drinking rum *mojitos* with two red-headed Czechs, and later Paula woke up in a small, strange bed, naked against Leandro's pocked back.

"I felt something different."

I was desperate to know exactly what they'd done, to be let in on the secret. Across the street by the bakery the Salmerón twins floated a paper boat on a green puddle, steering it with a stick, their white shirts buttoned up to their necks.

Paula said, "It's not like you're happy, because you're kind of sad. And alone. But you're at peace."

"Sounds like death," I said.

Paula smiled. "Except you know you're going to live a long, long time."

We walked on. I asked her some technical questions and she took her time answering, even if, as she said, there was no use in preparing me. Love forced on you a soppy amnesia, she told me, something like what she'd heard a doctor call an insult to the brain. I wasn't sure of this but felt we'd covered essential ground.

Paula's escape took several days to plan.

First we dug up Francisco Siete Rayo's magic beads in case Paula needed them. Then she "borrowed" some of Loló's loot that Mamá still kept under lock and key in Melena's spare room. This was not easy. There were a dozen keys on Mamá's key ring, some left over from the old Regla days. And Mamá had become an insomniac. She sometimes wandered the halls at night or sat in the dark parlor rocking.

Paula was mostly interested in Loló's jewelry, which she could sell on the black market. She kept an antique emerald wedding band for herself as an engagement ring. Leandro hid her bags in his attic. He had bought their train tickets and booked a hotel room for their honeymoon in the little seaside town of Baracoa.

Paula showed me what she'd get married in: the pale green muslin dress she'd worn the day she met Leandro at his *fiesta*. I couldn't say she seemed happy. But hers wasn't a reckless flight like Mamá's. Her eyes were clear. Her hands were warm.

That night we stood in the courtyard. Up in the black sky the moon was halved as if cut by a knife. Fyor slept, soothed by our voices and Paula's strokes on the back of his head.

"I'll send word when we're settled," she said.

I nodded. It occurred to me one could spend a life building a home, an elaborate nest for oneself in another person just to have somewhere to push from and flee.

Paula and I had done this.

We stood side by side facing the street. Paula took my hand and spun me around like a dance partner. I let her do it again and again.

When I stopped spinning, the earth was moving and Paula was running. At the end of the street she turned and waved. Her silver bracelets chingled.

17

THE MORNING after Paula left, Mamá woke up in the sunniest mood since the beginning of her "anemia." She got out of bed before I did and ran a bath with perfume and herbs like she used to in the tin basin of the Regla house. She said she was tired of the city. We would take a trip to the country, to Abuelita Carmen's, for some fresh air. Emanuel would come too. "He's spent enough time under the skirt of that old woman," Mamá said. "I want him to see the country, see other kids like him. The young girls in Cáceres will go wild. City boy, so serious and polite. Girls love that."

Mamá smiled. She massaged her skull with oil — worked her fingers back and forth fifty times. She said Mirta de Perales did this on TV when Mamá was a teenager. "When I was nineteen," Mamá said cheerfully, as if she and I had talked like this all month, "I dreamed of being a news reporter on television. There was only one lousy box for miles and it was at our neighbor Lydia's salon. I went on foot or sometimes jumped onto a wagon full of chickens. At the salon I swept hair, and Lydia had me water down the dyes from Havana so they'd last her the month. I did what she said so I could watch her television. We watched Mirta because she was a hairdresser and a *guajira* like us. We couldn't afford her flasks of gypsy oils and shampoos. But we admired her anyway."

Nelita walked in with the morning *café* and looked at our made bed. She was surprised by Mamá's sudden recovery. I wasn't. I knew Mamá's moods. She came out of the "darkness," as she called it, as if nothing had ever happened. I — and everyone else — was to join her in clever plans for the future. She had *el don*, Abuelita said once, the gift to sweep everyone along with her.

This morning Mamá looked me over and lifted my chin. "We'll go to the country," she repeated. She brushed her hair fifty strokes. Nelita dried Mamá's back harder now, to match Mamá's newfound energy.

"A letter came from Abuelita Carmen—she wants to see you." Mamá looked at me, watched the effect of her words.

I hadn't heard from Abuelita since my first weeks in the city when she'd sent a batch of *platanitos*. I'd written her a few letters but never heard back. Now Mamá fished an envelope from a drawer. "Elba from the grocery store writes for your *abuela*. Elba is *fuerte* now, a Party member. I know Mami can't say it but life has gotten hard for her in Cáceres. It'll do her good to see you."

I read the letter:

This is for la Tanya, my dear granddaughter, that I want for her to know I remember her always and for her to be careful in Havana with everything, to guard against the strong breeze of the bay at night. I have Elba read me her letters, how much she has grown, she sounds like a big *señorita, muy sabida y leida y escribida.*

Abuelita went on to other subjects, the people in the village, two deaths and one birth, the leaky roof and the lack of drinking water in the well. The letter was signed in an unreadable scribble.

Mamá sat next to me. "Literacy campaign," she said. "Your *abuela* can sign her name now."

We looked at the scribble and for the first time in months Mamá and I laughed together. She put her hand on my thigh and whispered, "*Frijolito,* I promise you, this trip will be marvelous."

But something in me—some old hurt—made me stiffen. Mamá never understood what I wanted. These promises hardened me. It didn't matter where we went. Life was difficult, everywhere and anywhere the same.

Once in school I saw a documentary about a young widow with six children washing clothes for a living, hands cracked and swollen. We were to learn from this what life was like before the Revolution. But what stuck with me was the mother's hard work, her steadiness and serious affection. Some part of me wished this from Mamá. I wanted her to make things work here, now. It was impossible. But whenever Mamá and I got this close, a small blade of hope cut me again.

18

OLD MELENA DIPPED her day-old bread into her *café con leche,* and when it was soft she brought it to her mouth. She licked her lips where the brown milk had stained, and dipped her bread again.

"Like I said, we'll only be gone a few weeks." Mamá smiled.

The old lady held her wet bread in midair and turned to Mamá. Her other hand reached for Emanuel's. "The boy's entrance exam is in two months. He's not finished with his Chopin. I have arranged for a tutor from the conservatory."

"Excuse me, Tia Petra, that's all very good but we are taking a family vacation."

Old Melena leaned over the table toward Mamá. "Mirella, what exactly is it you think Manuelito and I are doing? This is Manuelito's career."

Mamá lit a cigarette. Emanuel stared at his bean soup. "My congratulations to you on your hard work," Mamá said. "Now I think the kid needs a rest. The country air will do him good."

Old Melena set down her bread. "Mirella, do you ever consider what's best for this child?"

Emanuel slid from his chair, spoon in hand.

Mamá sat up. "What are you asking me, old woman?"

Emanuel looked at them, one and then the other. Before anyone could grab him, he was gone.

The nine o'clock cannon faded and Emanuel still had not come back. I was ordered to look for him. This came through Nelita from Melena's room where the old lady sat stewing in her juices and taking *tilo* for a migraine. I walked to the door but Mamá placed her arm, cigarette in hand, in my way. "Where do you think you're going?"

"Melena wants me to look for Emanuel. I can find him. I know his hideouts." I lied. I had no idea where he could have been. Still, I wanted to help.

Mamá shook her head. "One of you wandering the streets at night is enough." She sat down on the couch again. "I know my son. He's just blowing off steam. He's impulsive, like me. But he comes back."

We sat in darkness by the front window. I wondered if Mamá thought returning home was a virtue or a sin.

At a quarter to midnight, Emanuel opened the front door, then tried to shut it quietly. It hadn't rained outside, but his hair was wet as if he had just showered, and his sneakers were muddy.

I ran to him and hugged him, but in a moment Mamá grabbed him by the belt and in a clean flip she had him over her knees. She spanked him twice, loud. "You are my son," she said. "Remember that. You are my son and you do what I say."

Emanuel had just turned nine. He was still sweet and beautiful, the way boys are before they turn into long rough pack hounds. He looked at Mamá. He wasn't crying. Something about her words reassured him. Mamá got up and left the room.

I walked over to him. "I'm sorry you were alone," I said, and I was. I never lied to Emanuel.

"It didn't hurt." He rubbed his butt.

"I know. Mamá has no strength in her hands. I open jars for her." He smiled. I said, "Let's sleep outside tonight. Let's put blankets down in the courtyard by Fyor's spot." I held out my hand.

He paused. "Should we tell Melena?"

"You go on out. I'll send word with Nelita. Take sofa pillows with you."

For so long it was as if I'd forgotten Emanuel, given him up to his piano and Melena's attentions. Maybe I had been jealous, though I should have known better. Because what Mamá said was true. He would always be her son. And being Mamá's son was no great fate.

When I came back from Nelita's room, he was outside, already asleep next to Fyor, his dark curls resting on the pillow. I lay beside him and watched the black sky. The moon was like the two of us, vaguely full of something that was bright and good and that would not last.

19

IN THE three days Paula'd been gone, Mamá had washed our clothes by hand, starched and ironed each piece. She prepared for our trip, walking around the house with a pencil behind her ear, jotting down lists on scraps of paper she forgot by the kitchen sink or threw in the trash by mistake. Nelita searched the house for Mamá's misplaced lists.

One afternoon Mamá, Nelita and I sat side by side on the edge of our bed. Mamá wrapped a strand of my hair around a toilet paper tube. "The waves in your hair make you look like a dung beetle," she said. "Head too big for the body. Hair should hang down straight like a shower curtain."

It was two o'clock. Across the street the Moya and the CDR's monthly banner trembled out of focus in the glare of the afternoon sun. Women dragged rocking chairs out of their houses and faced the street in the cool of the porticos, no breeze but what they stirred rocking back and forth on the square tiles. Children and old people napped until three, a kinder hour to resume the day.

The doorbell rang. Nelita went to answer it and came from the parlor with her arms raised above her head as if a gun were poking at her back. "*Alejalo, Saint Alejo,*" she said. "The wizard."

Mamá jumped up from the edge of the bed. She assumed Loló's visit was for her. "Stay here," she said to me.

I had no intention of moving. A prayer came to me: "Eleggua *abrecaminos,* ruler of roads, close all paths of this world—" But I caught myself in time. Loló had more pull with the saints than I.

"He asks for *her.*" Nelita pointed in my direction. Mamá blinked. Then she stared at me, her nostrils wide.

I followed her to the parlor, where Loló stood behind the gray sofa. He had grown a beard and was dressed in full militia uniform. A gun in its shiny black case hung on his right hip. Old Melena sat still in the rocking chair, Emanuel next to her on the floor, butt on heels, arms crossed like a bodyguard.

"Paula is gone." Loló came around the sofa and stood before me. He blocked out the glare of the sun coming from the window. "She wrote a note to her mother. She's run away with someone." He paused. "Who? Who did this to her?" Loló's lips were almost white. His hands curled and uncurled. A good performance: concerned father defends daughter's honor—but his eyes gave him away. They were dark, anxious, more fearful than offended.

Mamá stepped forward. "I see you've joined the ranks." She fingered his olive green collar. He pushed her hand away. "The famous *babalawo,* mouthpiece of the saints, can't track down his own stepdaughter," Mamá said, her face placid. "*Que pasa,* Nicolás? The cowrie shells don't speak?"

"I don't know where Paula is," I said.

His thick hands opened and shut one last time. He took out a cigarette and lit it. "I see," he said. "Well." He turned to Mamá. "They're going to ship you back to that lunatic bin you came from. And quick." He snapped his fingers.

Mamá's smile faded. "Is that a divination or did you denounce me to your new buddies?"

He walked to the front door, opened it, turned back to me. "You should have cooperated, *chiquita.*" He said this with kind detachment, as if giving advice to one of his faithful clients.

As soon as Loló left, Nelita sprinkled water over her right shoulder to disinfect the house and drive out evil. Melena took Emanuel to bed. Mamá sat on the couch with her legs crossed, one foot shaking back and forth in the air. I thought of all that Loló had on us — the loot in the spare room, for one. He could accuse us of storing contraband, of black market dealings, and he'd have evidence, plenty of it, enough to send someone to jail for years.

The thought must have occurred to Mamá too because she stood and went to the spare room. In a moment glass broke against the floor. She didn't care who heard. She was rummaging through the loot, figuring out what was missing.

I went to our bedroom to consider my options. I could wander the streets like Emanuel or hide at Ruth Pendestal's, but I would only be putting off a fight and part of me wanted to get it over with.

"Congratulations," Mamá hissed when she finally came back to our bedroom. "You're in the big leagues now. You're not just an insolent know-it-all. Now you're a thief. You stole from your own mother."

"None of it was yours."

"It was in *my* safekeeping. It was *mine* to bargain with, *mine* to buy our freedom with." I realized then she'd always meant to steal it. Only I'd gotten to it first.

Mamá fell on me, grabbed a wrist in each hand and pinned me to the mattress. Her breath was sour. "Where's the jewelry?" She slapped me.

With my free hand I pulled her by the hair sideways until she fell to the floor. I jumped over her and ran out to the courtyard.

Old Melena, ghostlike in her nightgown, came outside. Mamá followed, pointing a shaking finger at me. The old lady stood between us.

"Get out of my way, Petra."

I looked at Mamá. "You knew what Loló did to Paula. You knew it all the time." This was my last test of Mamá's heart.

Mamá stopped and shut her eyes. She looked disgusted, not surprised. I had my answer. Mamá had suspected Loló. And still she had allowed him to touch her. Old Melena was right. Mamá made a shameful mess of life. She was a sad case.

The old lady stepped back. The myna bird Valentin, confused, shouted, "Good morning, good morning."

Mamá said to me, "Look at you gloat. You think my weakness justifies your cruelty." She opened her mouth again but said nothing, then turned and walked into the parlor. A moment later the front door closed and the cannon blast signaled nine o'clock.

Old Melena took me by the hand into the kitchen. She sat at the table and motioned for me to do the same. The skin on her face was almost translucent. An intricate maze of tiny blue veins crisscrossed her temples and cheeks.

"Start from the beginning, *niña*."

What was the beginning?

Melena stood. "Let's make some *tilo*. We need it, you and me." I lit the burner. The flame shot up suddenly, then found its level. Melena filled a pot with water. "What happened to Paula?" she finally asked.

I cleared my throat to buy time. But the old woman's blind faraway eyes had somehow settled on me. She was so still and attentive that I let loose with the whole tale. Aside from Leandro's hickeys and Paula's whereabouts I told her everything.

When I finished she said, "Breathe, *niña*. You live without breathing." I took in air and pushed it out. "Do it again," Melena said. "There's no charge for air." She paused. "Some people are called upon to carry strange burdens. You're one of them." I breathed again. She put her hand on my shoulder. "Let's see that spare room."

When Mamá and I had stored Loló's loot we had only been in the spare room with a flashlight. Now, under the bare bulb, I saw cobwebs hanging and roach droppings peppering the walls. Mamá had smashed all the empty jewelry jars. Clusters of broken glass covered the dark tiles.

What Paula and I hadn't bothered to steal was left untouched: tools and hunting knives and old framed pictures of dead relatives, an electric guitar, a flimsy Russian-made stereo with missing knobs. None of it was worth much, even on the black market. But at one time these knickknacks had been tokens of value to Loló from his clients, measures of their faith in the *babalawo's* power.

Melena held on to my elbow. She squeezed my arm hard at times and startled me.

"Go get some rice sacks from the kitchen and fill them with all this junk. All except those," she said, aiming her finger toward a pile of faded green leather-bound books in the corner. "That's my late husband's collection." She paused. "Go on, bring me a broom and dust pan."

I swept and Nelita threw away trash. What was left of Loló's loot filled twelve rice sacks. Only the leather-bound books remained, stacked neatly against the back wall. I stuck one of them, *Wuthering Heights,* under my shirt.

"Watch it, *niña,*" Melena said, her hand on my elbow. "My husband liked to read some filth—*A Thousand and One Nights*—very perverse. Take *Les Misérables.* Uplifting." I didn't want to read about miserable Frenchmen like Mamá did.

Hours later I woke on the old parlor couch, book open across my chest. I didn't remember falling asleep. A young man with narrow shoulders and stringy blond hair kissed Melena on the cheek and hauled the rice sacks out to an old Ford he'd backed to the gate. I wondered if he was one of Melena's mysterious protectors, one of her ex-students in high places. We stood at the gate and watched the car drive away.

I didn't know what Loló could still do to us now, with the loot gone, but Melena thought we were safe. "Come inside," she said to me. "They can't get us now."

On this last point the old lady was a romantic. She was hardly loved on our block. Last month, during the census, a question was asked of all households: Would we fight to defend the Revolution against its enemies? A yes answer was all that was required. But Melena said no, she would not. The interviewer pressed her. She said, "Young man, are you giving me a choice? If you are, you have my answer. If you're not, fill in whatever you like." The interviewer scribbled on his clipboard and all of September our CDR could not display the banner ONE HUNDRED PERCENT BEHIND YOU, FIDEL — a blot on our record caused, as the whole neighborhood knew, by an old stubborn windbag.

Melena was old and eccentric. She thought she had little to lose. I did not agree. To me anyone could lose anything anytime for any reason. This was what drew so many to faith and what turned others, like me, from it.

Now Melena walked a few steps toward the house. "I don't want to sleep with Mamá ever again," I said. She stopped. "Where will I sleep from now on?" I asked.

My question seemed to tire the old lady. She rubbed her eyelids.

"Where will I sleep from now on?" I repeated. I thought I could set up a cot in the spare room.

"My mother," Melena said, "didn't want me to marry. She wanted me to care for her and to sleep in her bed with her for the rest of her days. She was a widow, from Asturias." I remembered the haughty woman in the mantel photograph, her deepset eyes and straight mouth. "It took me years to figure out her intentions, but when I did, I married fast and left my mother's bed for good."

The old lady took my hand. My fingers stiffened a little in hers. She sighed. "With us," she said finally. "You sleep with us from now on. With your brother and me."

20

LOLÓ'S REVENGE came quickly.

The CDR president, Compañera Hilda, a paunchy woman with a permanent run in her stocking; Ruth Pendestal; and a tall young man, Compañero Andres from the "ministry" (he didn't say which one) came to our door in early November to run a "full inventory." Mamá went back to bed, since she was still "anemic" and on leave of absence from the matchbox factory. Melena held my hand and Emanuel's. Her lower lip shook as Nelita opened drawers and closets for Compañero Andres. He checked off Melena's possessions on a preprinted list of household objects.

By noon he'd taken away Melena's "ideologically diversionist" book collection and coins from her jewelry box (on one was the picture of a bearded yankee president).

Compañero Andres spoke quietly, with a slight lisp. His arms were tanned and hairy and his green eyes looked small behind his thick glasses. I never saw anyone more handsome. I wanted to hold his head against my chest and smooth down his thinning hair. He made me feel a strange compassion. But then I remembered what he was here to do to Melena, to all of us.

Everyone, even Mamá, sat with him around the kitchen table. He made his accusations sound like they were meant to do us good. He said the household "bordered on antisocial." I felt an odd sense of peace. Finally someone had passed judgment on our sins and given names to our trespasses. Now we'd be set right: Mamá would go to work and Emanuel and I would wear our blue pioneer scarves to school and each morning beneath the flag promise to "be like El Che." Our struggle would be the country's struggle—we would finally be like everyone else.

Compañero Andres said we must let Nelita go immediately: no servants were allowed in the Revolution. Nelita was to "work at a collective home where she and others of her capacity could contribute as the Revolution sees fit, each according to his ability."

Melena spoke. She was old, she said. She was blind. She could not understand the expectations of the new society.

"What concerns me, compañera," Andres said, "is the example we set for the children."

Melena winced as if a jungle *majá* had bitten her. "Stop it, *señor*," she said. "These children are more than well provided for."

Mamá stood up. "Excuse me, but I am the children's mother."

The young man turned his beautiful, detached face to Mamá. He shifted in his seat, then read more recommendations: weekly visits by the CDR president, Hilda, reports sent to the ministry outlining our progress and behavior in school, our nutritional and medical checkups and all "aspects of our formation." With each point, Compañera Hilda's head rose and fell in approval. "As for you" — Compañero Andres finally turned to Mamá — "you will report to a polyclinic at eight hundred hours and take a blood test. Then you will report to your work center, where your productivity will be closely monitored." It was a firm, polite order.

Compañero Andres rose and touched my head and Emanuel's with the kindness of a priest. Compañera Hilda and Ruth Pendestal followed him out. Nelita closed the front door.

When she came back to the kitchen, Nelita gave Melena a piece of paper with a phone number. "The man said I should keep this in case someone tries to confuse me," Nelita said. "Who's going to confuse me?"

The old lady's eyes were wet. Emanuel hugged her shoulders. He too was crying. I looked at Melena and Nelita and could not catch my breath.

"Look what you've done. Are you happy yet?" Mamá grabbed my arm.

Melena said, "Silence! Everyone quiet. I must think what to do."

"Nobody's going to confuse me," Nelita said. "Who's going to confuse me?"

Mamá let go of my arm and I fell forward. Emanuel tried to pull me up, but I wanted to sit there, on the floor. I had set off a chain of catastrophes, this time on my own, without the help of saints or devils. On the shiny tiles under me, my face stared back, gray and flimsy like a ghost's.

21

MELENA'S CONTACTS in high places told us to bide our time. Compañero Andres was a protégé of Celia Suarez, Fidel's "companion." He was impossible to bribe. If we had any pull with the saints, this was the time to use it. But we had none. And Melena's sagging Jesus seemed too caught up in his own suffering to ease ours.

Early Tuesday, I helped Nelita pack her belongings in boxes. She didn't have much and I took my time, folding the clothes neatly and wrapping her hollow ceramic elephant in old newspaper. She grabbed a photo of Alfredo Nilan the Beautiful out of my hand and placed it on top of the knapsack, so it wouldn't be crushed. From her windowsill, three little saint statues looked on. Half hidden in shadows, they seemed to smile, as if sharing a joke. I thought I saw Eleggua, the trickster, wink.

After packing, Nelita sat in the parlor, rocking, saying her "*Alejalo, Saint Alejo*" refrain over and over like a prayer. Melena and I sat with her. Outside a drizzle soaked the pavement but the sun shone through. Melena muttered, "Sun and rain and the devil's daughter gets married."

Nelita's sister Dora, from El Cerro, showed up around noon. She sat on the couch and sipped *café* as if she were here for an ordinary visit. After some chitchat, she and Melena rose but Nelita stayed put, rocking. Her big head hung down. Melena and Dora whispered in her ear, and she finally stood. Melena led her to the door. "No crying," the old lady told her at the steps. She held Nelita's broad face with both hands. "Remember what I said. You'll be back here. Soon." Melena kissed her assistant slowly on both cheeks. Nelita rocked from side to side. Mamá came from the bedroom and kissed Nelita's forehead quickly, without looking, the way you kiss a body at a wake. Nelita cringed. She held the door frame and grunted, paused, then wailed from deep in her belly.

Melena tried to shush her—neighbors were coming to their doors—but Nelita threw her head back, eyes closed, and cried louder. With her backside she butted the old lady, who stumbled into me and crushed my foot. Dora squeezed Nelita's shoulders and repeated, "Behave yourself now, you know what'll happen if you don't." But Nelita didn't budge. Dora pried her sister's stubby fingers one by one from the door. For each finger she pulled, Nelita put the others back stronger. Dora clenched her teeth and sank her long nails into Nelita's fleshy left hand. Nelita let go, in pain, and Dora pulled her down the steps onto the street.

Melena shut the front door. Nelita's screams could still be heard.

Part Two

22

THE LAST BLOCK MEETING of 1967 was held in the CDR hall, a pre-Revolution cafeteria with greasy curtains and a ceiling blackened by kitchen fires. Nelita sat in the front row of backless benches. She shot little glances at Alfredo Nilan the Beautiful who stood, oblivious, in the back. Next to Nelita sat her sister, Dora, in a starched linen blouse, a pink embroidered D over her heart. I squeezed myself between Mamá and Ruth Pendestal in the third row. We'd only attended three meetings that year, excused from most of them by Melena's blindness or Mamá's "anemia." Even now that Nelita's fate would be decided, Melena had refused to come. She expected "nothing but cruelty" from her country's government and stayed home with Emanuel, who read to her from the weekly church newsletter, *La Vida Cristiana*.

All that winter Dora visited us and weighed us down with complaints. She didn't want Nelita in her home. Dora had no patience for Nelita's ways of mourning, her moans and mutterings and Saint Alejo panics. Dora loved her sister, but not enough to live with her. During her visits Dora brought illegal candy she'd made at home to sell—"on the side, you understand." She winked. Emanuel and I sucked on the burnt sugary squares as Dora kept fishing, seeing if Melena or Mamá had any hidden contacts they could bring to the case. Finally Mamá promised to talk to Ruth Pendestal, who could raise the issue with the neighborhood council and have Nelita returned to us.

Now in the CDR hall, Compañera Hilda, brown ankle peeping from a hole in her stocking, opened the meeting with the latest volunteer figures. She stood up behind the head table—several long boards raised from the floor by stacks of bricks—and shook her head after each number. "Compañeros, the leadership has issued projections for next year's sugar crop. Our commander in chief has issued a challenge: ten million tons of sugar. Compañeros, this Revolution benefits everyone. Everyone must step forward. This block is mobilized!"

She paused for applause, then shook her hand at us to stop. "Now. Mothers complain to me. They say they can't leave their houses and their children to volunteer to cut cane on Sundays. What is to be done? It doesn't take much to solve this." She locked her hands behind her back, then said, "The older compañeros, those who are ill, those who can't help with the harvest— *they* will contribute by watching the block's children on Sundays." She was interrupted by applause again, even from the old people she'd just singled out for babysitting.

The floor opened then for the night-watch schedule. Compañero de Silva, the old secretary, scribbled on his pad. From time to time Compañera Hilda, now sitting at the head table, whispered to a skinny woman beside her. This woman wasn't from the neighborhood. She glanced at her watch as if she was bored.

Next to me Ruth Pendestal squirmed. After Compañera Hilda announced that brooms had arrived and streets would be swept each Thursday evening, Ruth raised her hand and described Melena's situation. She asked whether the committee would consider "Compañera Petra's case" and issue an exception; whether they would allow Nelita to return.

The bored woman on stage rose from her seat and the CDR president introduced her as a ministry representative. "If I may," the woman started, "there is a shortage of housing on the island. A real crisis. Compañera Petra needs help. No?"

Ruth Pendestal nodded. Mamá cupped her mouth and mumbled, "Oh God, no."

The ministry woman held up several long pieces of paper. "I have a list here of two hundred and fifty families waiting for places to live. As Compañera Presidente stated, everyone benefits from the Revolution. It is imperative that everyone contribute to our country's future. Many of the families here"—she raised the list again—"include grandparents who are happy to offer companionship and to help Compañera Petra with her chores. This would be required of them, of course, as a condition for moving in." Compañera Hilda's head bobbed up and down.

Ruth gave it one last try. "Will Nelita return to Compañera Petra's house also?"

My stomach hurled up, then sank back into gravity the way an elevator starts and stops, that sudden pull to earth.

With a flick of the hand, the CDR president motioned for Ruth to sit. The ministry leader said, "Compañera, *por favor*, the need to help Compañera Petra has been addressed. There are other pressing items here. If you have further concerns, take them up with the leadership at a later time."

Ruth sat down. President Hilda cleared her throat and began assigning volunteers to chop sugar cane in the year of the ten million tons.

23

SOMEONE KNOCKED on our front door in the middle of a rainstorm, and a sixtyish-year-old woman came into the parlor in a dripping raincoat. She was short and swollen, so fat she looked almost square. The corners of her mouth curved down as if in permanent distaste for life. Melena introduced her to us as Señora Cacha. "Cachita," the woman corrected her, "Cachita Guevara. No relation."

Her grown children, Pilar and Moises, scooted back and forth, hauling three nylon-covered cots and a dresser past us into Nelita's old bedroom and the spare room. Mamá, Melena, Emanuel and I stood in the parlor and watched them muddy up the floor. We watched Pilar's baby, Richard, slip on the wet tiles and land on his butt. We didn't move. On Melena's orders we were not to lift a finger when they came. The parakeets sang and shrieked.

Why did the Guevaras have to move in now, in the rain? The house would still be here when the weather cleared. Later we found out their old crumbling building had collapsed in a thunderstorm like this one. They'd lost most of their things.

Moises stuck his head into the parlor to ask Melena's permission to move the parakeet cages that sat above the baby's crib in the hallway. He was tall and thin and his pale hands hung down. Melena said nothing to him. Mamá went to help Moises, and when she came back she informed us he was a film student at the university and had even been on television. Mamá said this with pride — as if we now lived with a celebrity.

Melena said, "Your son will be on television before you know it, and not for carrying on like a clown but for his great, gifted playing."

"Sure," Mamá said. Emanuel looked up at her. "Nothing against your playing, *mi niño,* but getting on TV is not easy." She left the room. Emanuel crossed his legs and rounded his back like a snail coiling into itself.

The Guevaras' presence spread like gas. Cachita was always busy. Early mornings on her walks home from the bakery she picked up odds and ends littered along the sidewalks or beside trash bins — bows and ribbons and a strange hood ornament — and she hung them, scrubbed clean, as decorations above the baby's crib. She had the practical *resolver* spirit of the country — making use of every last thing, even trash. She made thick stews from leftovers and the smells drowned out the aroma of Melena's *café con leches.*

Señora Cachita's first test of strength came over the piano. Emanuel banged at it day and night. At first Cachita pointed to the sheet music and said, "That kid'll ruin his sight playing those little black notes." Then, "His fingers will fall off!" She eyed the piano suspiciously—a big noisy thing that did nothing but take up space.

Without asking anyone, she and Pilar dragged it from under the window to a corner one night to make room for their altar to Ochún and the few costumed dolls Pilar had salvaged from their old house. We woke to a new parlor. Emanuel went on playing in his corner as if nothing had been touched.

Next Cachita put cotton balls in her ears and sometimes sent Pilar to clean the piano when Emanuel sat down to play. He waited patiently beside Pilar as she scrubbed the ivory keys with a wet cloth. When she was done he wiped the keys with the inside of his shirt but his fingers still slipped as he played.

After another washing of the keys, Melena finally stepped in. "Manuelito is not to be disturbed," she said to Pilar. But her voice wavered. Those days she seemed pale and small and wandered the house lost, "a soul in purgatory," as she put it. Only four pupils came by for lessons now. "Who can blame the others," the old lady had said to me. "Ruth told the world I even needed help to pee."

Only Moises and Mamá were friendly. She ambushed him in the parlor late afternoons when he got home from the university and tried to charm him with her sophisticated gloom. She seemed in need of distraction after her matchbox factory days. Her face covered in makeup, her hair teased, she sat casually in the parlor. Moises clowned with her, but his eyes stayed cool. He was wary of Mamá. He told her she always looked "like a bomb about to go off."

Mamá laughed a little too loud at this. She seemed shocked. All these efforts to seem interesting, not just eccentric and troubled, came to nothing.

If people ever saw through Mamá, few told her so. Even me. After I'd turned eight, I'd begun to suspect that Mamá's dramas and plans for escape were all that kept her afloat. That at any second she could go under. There was a darkness around her, a recklessness that scared me. Sometimes crossing the street as a child, I held her hand but kept my eyes on the road in case I had to pull us to the curb. When I turned twelve, I sometimes imagined letting the hand go, making my own way.

After her last chat with Moises, Mamá walked up to me in the kitchen, her eyes underlined with dark rings. She asked that I bring a dinner tray to her room in the evenings.

For days we didn't see her. I left the dinner tray by her locked door and picked it up in the mornings once she'd gone to work. She had nibbled at the bread and drunk the *café* but Cachita's thick stews sat mostly untouched, an occasional upturned fly on top.

After a week Mamá finally came out to the parlor and moved about the house like a cat, gliding through doorways, eyes opened big—bigger, it seemed, than ever before.

I sat next to her on the couch and showed her one of Moises' books full of illustrations, of scenes from plays and silent yankee movies. I thought they'd please her, but the red-carpeted movie sets, rich with fake gold and painted skies, seemed to make her suffer. To her the pictures were proof of what existed *afuera*, on the outside, beyond her reach. "It had to be my luck," she said, "to get stuck on a shipwrecked island like this fellow here." She pointed to a picture of Robinson Crusoe holding a ratty umbrella over his head.

That evening I went to her door with the dinner tray. She was gone but the door was open and I stepped inside. Mamá was the only one in the house who still had a room and a double bed to herself. The rest of us were packed tight like canned Russian meat, three cots squeezed side by side in the bedrooms. Mama's bed was unmade, her bras and worn panties on the floor. Dust and the stink of smoke covered everything. I set the tray down on the floor. There, next to the bed, a glint of silver caught the sunlight. I looked closer. A crucifix gleamed upside down in a wineglass full of water, a folded note under the glass. I pulled the paper out. It was soft, curled in at the corners, as if it had been folded and refolded many times. The note was a wish, the wish Mamá had, always: "*Virgencita*, grant me a safe passage."

Where was she going this time? The word "safe" made me think the passage had been arranged—only the safety was in question. I slid the paper back under the glass.

When I came out of the room Mamá was pacing in the courtyard. She said, "You're looking tall these days," but her eyes went through me. She hadn't really looked at me at all.

24

PAULA CAME BACK during Lent, as streamers and empty bottles were carted off our street from the latest CDR cane-cutting celebration.

Melena brought *café* out to the parlor as if we were grown-ups. She sat on the couch with Mamá, across from Paula and me. Paula's ironed hair was rolled in a bun and she looked at least twenty. Her bracelets were gone. She wore tiny diamond earrings.

"I just dropped by," she said carefully, "to tell you we're back from Baracoa, from our honeymoon." She lingered on the last word. She wanted Melena and Mamá to know she was married.

"Oh, Baracoa," Mamá sighed. "I went there once. Not too far from Cáceres. So quaint."

I thought of how Paula would soon slip out of her wifely costume and we'd sit on the stoop elbow to elbow like we used to. But she talked on about Leandro's new job in his father's office. Melena and Mamá sat stiff, eyes to the floor.

Paula flashed her long pearly fingernails left and right,

and something in me started to hate her. She seemed full of things I didn't know, full of boasting and parading. Maybe I'd been a fool stealing for her and facing Loló's wrath for her, ruining Nelita's and Melena's life just so Paula could come here in her finery and sip *café* like a *gran señora*.

Finally Paula stood. Melena and Mamá got up too and gave her little kisses on the cheek.

Mamá said to me, "What's with you? Get up and see your friend to the door. Aren't you two nail and flesh?"

Paula gave me her hand. "Come. I have something to show you, Flesh."

But there was nothing more of hers I wanted to see.

Paula was a mule, as Mamá said once, and she pulled me up with her skinny arms and dragged me past the piano, through the door and down the front steps. She whispered, "I want you to see our apartment in El Focsa," and squeezed my arm with her creamy nails. "We'll look at the moon from my balcony."

I didn't answer. Paula was living in a high-rise overlooking the ocean. We'd lost our home to strangers.

She undid her bun. Her ironed hair stood straight out from her head and she looked at me. "It's me, *chica*," she said. "It's me."

We walked to the corner of our street. A group of men were standing there, talking *beisbol*. Behind us at the Moya, Carina may have been painting her toenails on the stairs, Loló watching her. For all I knew Paula had already paid her respects there, the three of them sitting around the kitchen table, one big happy family.

Paula set her hand on my arm again. I yanked it away.

"What *is* with you?" she said. I kicked her shin. She kicked back.

A little man with raccoon teeth stepped away from the group at the corner and said, "Don't fight, *niñas*. I'll take you both." The others laughed.

I said to Paula, "You can go to hell."

The man came closer. "*Niñitas*, please. Just kiss and make up like good girls."

"Fuck off," Paula said and spat in his direction. That almost made me forgive her.

The men laughed again. The air smelled of hair-straightening lotion, Paula's smell.

"It wasn't me," Paula said. "Loló did it. He got your inventory started."

"I want things back . . ." I said. "To how they were. Before." I was going to cry.

She waited a moment. "Things weren't so good before."

Our skirts brushed in the breeze. We pulled back, the air between us tingly and nervous like fingers.

25

ONE AFTERNOON on my way home from school I saw
Compañero Andres standing across from the Moya. He
wiped the bald spot at the back of his head with a handkerchief. Then he called me over and we shook hands.
"I've come to pay you a visit, if you don't mind," he said.

In the parlor he took off his glasses and polished them
with the same handkerchief. I walked past him to get Melena but he gave me a sad, little-boy smile and motioned
for me to sit on the rocking chair. He eased himself down
onto the edge of the couch. His face looked younger now,
maybe twenty-five. His eyes were bigger without the thick
lenses.

"I want to ask," he said, "whether the situation is better
here, now that you have others to help with the chores."

Was the ministry looking for gratitude? I said, "Chores
were never a problem."

Glasses back on, he studied me. I felt dirty in my uniform, sweaty from running laps at school. Compañero
Andres's white shirt was starched. His black shoes shone.

He fingered Moises' book on the coffee table. "We'll arrange for you to read more serious books that have a positive impact. Tell me, what would you like to be, as they say, when you grow up?"

I knew enough to answer, "Whatever the Revolution needs."

"The Revolution needs many things. If you like to read, that's good." He looked at the book again. "But let me be frank with you. I've been in touch with your teachers. They say you're bright but you don't excel. That you have the capacity but not the desire."

I wanted to change the subject. "My brother Emanuel, he's a pianist. He's going to take the entrance exam to the conservatory—"

"Then he doesn't need my help." He leaned forward. "Before the Revolution poor children like you had no chance. You know that. Young women weren't expected to contribute, to become scientists, technicians, engineers. That's changed now." He looked around the room, his green eyes sparkling. "We are living in the best time of history, a time when someone like you can have any fate she desires. *Comprendes?*" He looked straight at me. "Your teachers say you're smart. And I see how you're looking at me now. You're thinking all the time."

I tried not to nod. But it was good to be seen. To be seen kindly.

He leaned forward again, almost out of his seat. "You don't want to just live. Am I right? You want a good fate, something to live *for*. The Revolution guarantees a worthy life. But you need to take the necessary steps."

I saw a long staircase leading to my chosen fate. What that would be, I didn't know. But what if I wasn't a shipwreck on some lost island? What if no Virgin had to grant safe passage? What if there were enough good fates right here, ready for the picking?

Compañero Andres held out his hand. "Tanya," he said. He hadn't said my name before. "Friends?" I nodded. "Thank you. I'll do my best to deserve it."

We were standing, though I didn't remember getting up. He looked at his watch. The parlor, crowded with Ochún and the dolls and the cornered piano, now felt like a storage closet, some temporary stop I'd laugh about later once I'd reached my real fate. Compañero Andres said, "Please go get your mother."

"Mamá's at work." It was barely four o'clock.

He looked down at his shiny shoes. "Please don't worry," he said finally, "but your mother is not at work today. She hasn't been there all week."

"She's ill," I said.

Compañero Andres shook his head. "Tanya, you must understand this: In a historical process some people are left behind. They can't be dragged along." He turned to the door. "Tell your mother I stopped by."

Wait a minute, I wanted to say. But there was no use. He'd left me the same old fate I'd always had, the one I'd never chosen: to give Mamá up, each time a little further, not just in words but in the heart, not just in the heart but in the world.

26

I LEANED OVER Mamá's crucifix, squeezing her note to the Virgin in my hand. It was six in the evening. The food tray was rancid from the night before. I picked it up from the floor. Mamá was standing inside the doorway.

"Fifteen," she said and slid the door shut with her foot. "You're about to turn fifteen. In this place." She walked to her chair covered with dirty clothes and plopped herself down. "I used to make plans for your fifteenth birthday. A party. A long dress. But my plans turned to smoke." She signaled to the thin strip from her cigarette, then looked at me hard. "You helped turn them to smoke, you know." She meant her nest egg, Loló's loot. I walked to the door as she said, "I'm turning into a real factory hand, you know? A perfect *obrera*. On the other hand, you . . ." She paused. "*Ah si*, we were talking about you. Your Fifteens. What would you have liked?" I had no answer for this. She got up and looked out the window. "You were a stubborn child. Kept counsel in your own little head. I always felt you . . . watching." She stopped, as if she'd come to some revelation. "You watch me, don't you? That's the worst thing about you. Like this whole country, you've grown eyes in the back of your head—those dog eyes you got from your father." She sucked in air. "You look at me as if all of this"—she opened her arms—"is my fault."

I set the tray on the bed. My arms couldn't hold it.

"I bet the old lady has you saying rosaries, the two of you on your knees every night." Mamá clasped her hands together. "I can just see you. Praying to the angels for a new mother. Some Cachita-type rummaging through trash bins—"

"I don't want that." Mamá looked at me. I said, "You don't show up to work. Compañero Andres came looking for you." Mamá's big eyes were steady, piercing. She seemed like a rudder suddenly snapped back into whack.

"What *do* you want?" she asked. Mamá waited. She could be patient when she felt like it.

"I want to trust you," I said finally. It sounded like a whine.

"And you can't." Mamá slapped her thigh, her eyes mocking. "*Pobrecita.* Tell me something. Was it you they dragged to a rehabilitation center? Was it you they slapped around? Did you sleep with their slogans in your ears? Did your children get parceled out to strangers? You don't trust me but you trust your Compañero Andres, as you call him."

"I want to know what you're doing skipping work."

"You want to know! You come in here snooping around for those motherfuckers and you can't trust me! You, clutching my personal papers in your hand and you don't trust *me?*" She paused. "I fight hard for you. And you're ready to throw me to the first shark that comes circling. You want to get rid of me!" She grabbed me by the shoulders. "What would you be without me?"

I let her shake me.

"You refuse to understand where you live." She let me go and her voice softened. "In another place you wouldn't betray your mother like this. You wouldn't have to. In another place you'd be different. I'd be different." We sat on the unmade bed. Mamá stroked my back with her open palm. "*Mi frijolito,* your father's been in touch with me. I can't say more, but things are right this time."

I crushed her note in my palm. I didn't believe her. "In another place" was Mamá's broken record. I didn't believe in yankee paradises. Nor did I think crossing an ocean would make us better than we were.

Her hand dropped from my hair and she looked off again. "I know you don't want to leave. I don't either. But leaving might be the only destiny for those born on small islands."

I looked at her.

She smiled. "I read it somewhere."

Her note slipped from my hand to the floor. Neither of us picked it up.

27

MY TRUCE WITH MAMÁ didn't last. Love between us came with rage and long-standing grudges. Love did us no good. For a few days we pretended it did. Mamá softened and gave friendly orders—wash this, iron that, and for that time, I did what she said.

The weather turned dry, and whenever the strong Lent wind rattled the shutters, Mamá would jump. Sometimes she grabbed my hand and her fear shot up my arm and down my spine. She wanted me to feel it.

That week CDR president Hilda herself delivered a box sealed with a Ministry of the Interior stamp. Inside were *The Communist Manifesto, History Will Absolve Me* and *Elementary Odes,* and a note that read: "Just to get you started—Have fun, Andres." Mamá saw the books and the note and gave me a look full of dark questions. Moises leaned over the box, turning up his nose at the *Manifesto.* "Girl, is this a suitor or someone who wishes you ill?"

Mamá looked at me. "Does he think you're his little student? His disciple?" Moises smiled but Mamá brooded.

Since our talk in her room, she'd thought of me as a co-conspirator. I'd let her down. Again.

"These types need disciples, little adoring fans," Moises said.

"Don't fall for this," Mamá started. She kept talking fast in her low, mocking tone. I heard Moises' little hen clucks as I left for the courtyard.

He followed me, carrying my box, and put it down next to me and Fyor. "Don't singe your eyebrows with that *caca* day and night."

He left and I fingered the yellowed pages of the *Odes*. Day and night, I thought. All day and all night.

28

THREE WEEKS after Paula's return I finally went to see her apartment in El Focsa. Everything in it was white: the tile floors, the walls, the plastic table and chairs, the Italian leather couch Paula said was a present from Leandro's mother. Over the couch Paula and Leandro had hung a picture of their wedding day in Baracoa, the little eastern port where Columbus first set foot on the island and said, "This is the most beautiful land human eyes have ever seen."

From Paula's balcony I tried to see what he'd meant. The strong light, even at day's end, bathed buildings and people in a strange brilliance, as if the rooftops and crumbling storefronts along the seawall were lit from within. The ocean's blue seemed painted on, fantastic. It made me feel like a visitor: the light and the ocean would stay forever and I would pass on, swallowed up in them.

Paula came out to the balcony with two tall glasses of *champola,* full of tiny ice cubes. The drink was milky and sweet. In that fierce light her skin seemed brighter. Was it

Leandro's caresses that brought blood to the surface? I'd smelled Leandro's aftershave in the bathroom, his sweat in the hanging towels. I'd peeked at their unmade bed. The sheets were crumpled, as if Paula and Leandro lived in their bed while the rest of us only slept in ours.

Paula and I leaned on the balcony rail. "Somewhere down there with all the ant people," she said, "he eats and sleeps and breathes. There are days when I think, I'll make a phone call"—she snapped her fingers—"and off he goes to La Cabaña Prison or to chop cane for the rest of his life."

"You won't do anything," I said.

Paula looked at me, surprised.

"You won't."

I believed this. I believed of all people, Paula would walk through evil and refuse to touch it. She'd come out of it radiant and unchanged, a little like Melena's Jesus walking through the waves. It was crazy. But to me each person should have someone believe this of them. For Paula I was it.

Paula shrugged. "I don't call because of my mother."

Carina had done nothing to keep Loló away from Paula. "Your mother opened her legs and pushed you out. That's all," I said.

"She's my mother."

Once in Melena's church, Padre Llerena had said, "Honor thy father and mother." He didn't say to love them. He said honor them. Was Paula doing this? I wasn't big on laws or commandments, but I'd probably broken this one and might break it again if I had to.

Paula said, "I'm sorry about Melena's house." Her hand lay next to mine on the railing. Her nails were eaten, the pearly enamel bitten off in parts. "I'm sorry I couldn't help you." She brushed back her hair. "We'll get you out of there soon."

The sun scraped the sky red on its way to the water. I was waiting for the old Paula to show up, bracelets chingling. I wanted to say, "Let's go back to my old stoop and watch the moon, and at the cannon blast you run home." But home to what?

The front door opened and Leandro burst in. They kissed, then kissed again. He said, "Chini, I brought steaks from Mami's." Paula took a package from him and went to the kitchen.

Tiny holes covered Leandro's cheeks and neck, scars from some war he must have won. With the acne went his shyness. He came at me, arms extended. "Sit down, *chica*, sit down. You're family here."

From her new candle-bright kitchen (no one on the island escaped the blackouts), Paula smiled. She cooked her steaks on the kerosene burner.

She was right. Things hadn't been so good before.

29

By march Mamá's dinner tray ritual was over. I left her food warming on the stove and she ate from the open pots, late at night. She dropped all talk of leaving the island, even of visiting the countryside. After work she locked her door behind her and went on long, mysterious outings.

One Saturday afternoon Emanuel asked her where she was going and Mamá said she was volunteering at her work center. I smiled at the joke but she shot me a look of hatred. "I don't see why you should be surprised. You, who give *everything* to the Revolution."

My face burned, even though I didn't know what she meant. It wasn't till Monday I figured out she had been referring to Andres and I wanted to spit in her garlic soup that night.

All that week Cachita had only served us garlic soup and bread. She was punishing us for Sunday, when she'd fallen and landed face up on the kitchen floor, short legs and arms struggling to turn her body. No one had rushed to help her; the commotion sounded to us like her daily scuffles with Pilar—the two chasing each other up and down the hall, arguing over how many drops of hydrogen peroxide would lighten Pilar's hair, or how many buckets it took to flush the toilet. Sometimes Pilar was calm and Cachita screamed, other times Pilar started the fights. They took turns in some order only they understood. Whenever Melena's blindness got her in their way Cachita grabbed the old lady by the shoulders—so fragile and light was Melena now—and moved her to the side.

But last Sunday Cachita claimed Melena bumped into her and tripped her. "On purpose," she said as Emanuel bent over and helped her up. "She stood there and tripped me." She pointed to a spot near the leaking refrigerator. Cachita's gray hair stuck out from its shell combs.

Old Melena's face was red and excited. "If you hadn't pushed me, your feet wouldn't have tangled with mine and landed you on your behind."

"So you admit it," Cachita said.

"You pick me up in my own house and throw me in corners like I was a dust rag." Melena blinked, suddenly fierce as in the old days. "I'm old and blind but this is *my* house." She pounded her chest.

"This house," Cachita said, "is a multiple family dwelling."

"Maybe you slipped." Emanuel turned to the puddle by the refrigerator.

"This doesn't end here." Cachita shuffled up to Melena, then jerked her canvas bag from the floor and limped off.

Their war escalated. The old lady claimed furniture was

moved in the night so she'd bump into it in the morning and break her skull; Cachita accused Melena of throwing the Ochún candles in the garbage. I told Melena to stop the nonsense. Cachita could easily spit in our stew—I knew how tempting this was. Worse, she could register a formal complaint with the CDR, and another intervention would finish us.

We felt close to finished already that spring—not just us but the whole country. The drive for the ten million tons came to nothing—even the comandante had said so on TV. And suddenly everyone woke up as if from a dream: Ten million tons of sugar had been an impossible, even crazy, goal. And now, after diverting all resources and manpower to it for a year, the country was stripped. Rations tightened. Everywhere black market operators sprang up, each more expensive than the last, and they all wanted pesos, not condensed milk cans. Melena's cash supply grew thin. She was down to two pupils (forty pesos a month). That and Mamá's sixty pesos could only buy us a couple weeks' worth of meals.

The old lady sold some of her mother's jewelry. A gold chain and medallion were worth fifty pesos and we bought rice, eggs, *café*, a few thin steaks and powdered milk. Together we searched her drawers, setting aside silver spoons and candle holders, silk hankies, gold cufflinks from her late husband, to be sold as needed.

Meanwhile she sent me off to trade and deal after school, mostly in the Moya. I was known there, so my visits were not suspicious to the CDR. On the third floor lived a lady who sold rice and lard, and a few doors down, a man who stole steaks from his job at a meat plant. Meat went bad during the blackouts, and he gave away some bargains. Doña Luisa in 207 didn't drink *café* and sold her rations to the highest bidder. She was expensive, but Melena lived on *café con leches* and we paid her price.

I was most afraid of seeing Loló there. I watched his apartment door, and if Carina was in the courtyard hanging clothes I went around back and ran up the stairs breathless, heart pounding, three steps at a time.

One evening near the end of August, Loló came up the steps as I was rushing down with my canvas bags. He was in full military uniform with big black boots and a pistol hanging at his side. His giant hand squeezed the railing, fat and puffed up like a boxing glove. From the neck down he was a slow-moving bull, but his head tilted and turned quickly like a bird's. His eyes found my face and he smiled.

"What brings you around here, *chiquita*?" He looked at my bags.

I backed up the stairs toward Doña Luisa's.

"And how is your dear mother?" he shouted at me. "Still on the loose?"

That afternoon when I came home, my arms gave off the rotting-onion stink of panic. The old lady didn't notice. She took my bags and sat me down across the kitchen table for one of our whispered head-to-head debriefings.

"How much for sugar?" she asked.

"Ten pesos."

"That old thief."

"Doña Luisa sits on it. Sugar doesn't go bad."

"The world's biggest sugar grower, and there isn't a spoonful to go around." Melena poured me some water. "They give it to the Russians, *niña*. Everything good goes to the Russians."

The old lady patted my hand. She treated me like the breadwinning husband. I knew how much money we had. It was up to me to make it last the month.

30

ON MY FIFTEENS I brought Paula a piece of birthday cake.

That morning Mamá wore an apron for the first time in years and made custard like she used to in Regla. She poured in most of our month's ration of condensed milk. The four of us and the Guevaras gathered around the kitchen table.

Moises licked his spoon. "Gemini?" he asked me.

"A ram," Mamá smiled. "Big hard head. A ram." With her long bangs, the dark rings under her eyes, hands in the pockets of her African print housedress, Mamá looked like a deposed princess making do in some unbearable exile.

Melena gave me an old pearl necklace from her mother's stash and Emanuel a copper pin he'd made himself at the school shop. I wore them that evening when Paula took me to Karachi, a dark basement club where the leadership got drunk nights. Leandro was out of the city on official business with his father and she invited me to sleep over. Karachi was not much bigger than Melena's court-yard. Lanterns hung from the ceiling. Young women stood against the back wall, arms crossed, smiling, peering into the faces of the men leaning over them. Paula and I were by far the youngest there.

We chose a table toward the back and Paula pointed out friends of her in-laws and other acquaintances—some of them drunks, she whispered, smugglers, secret counter-revolutionaries, *gusanos* waiting to defect like El Gambao. Any one of them could leave on an official trip and not return.

"While I'm young," Paula said, "I want to travel. I hope Leandro's father sends us abroad. I'd even go to Albania." She smiled and looked up from her drink. "I'd miss you, *chica*. But I want to see the world."

Some people didn't get enough of the world. They chased after it like a train they'd missed.

"My mother tells me you have a suitor," Paula said. "The whole CDR knows. People call him the Stiff Little Clerk."

"He's not a suitor. He's at least twenty-eight."

She shrugged. To her a man's interest in a young girl was a thing of nature. Grown men had chased Paula since she turned eleven. Strangers followed her for blocks, nos-trils wide, almost angry, as if she owed them something.

"Maybe you'll meet someone here," she said, scanning the crowd. "We have to do something about your situa-tion." She wanted me to follow in her footsteps—marry up into the inner circle. I reminded her she'd fallen in love.

But Paula put on a teacherly smile and waved someone

to our table, a man she introduced as Frankie. "He works in the Mexican embassy," she told me. Frankie's black hair was slick and wavy. He shook my hand but kept his eyes on Paula. They talked and laughed and Paula threw back her head and laughed again. Frankie was some comedian.

On the small dance floor they spun and circled their hips. Frankie stood slightly bow-legged and thrust his pelvis forward as he moved toward Paula, who stood in place to meet him. I swallowed my beer fast. It tasted bitter like medicine.

They came back panting. "Who died at this table?" Paula said to me. Frankie lit a cigarette and passed it to Paula, who looked around the place and puffed smoke through her nostrils. She smiled at Frankie. "It's her Fifteens tonight," she said.

They looked at me. I blushed. Paula and I stood and made our way to the bathroom through a gauntlet of perfumed, slick-haired men. Inside, Paula half smiled, amused. "You were looking at me out there," she said. "Like I'm a slut or something."

"You're drunk," I said.

But could I help looking? Paula was the best I'd seen in people. Why should she work so hard to become a fake?

"Do you like this Frankie?" I asked.

"Oh," she said, as if she'd never considered it. And I understood then that this was a kind of transaction. Paula was showing me a new way to trade. Her looks were her currency and she could barter them as she wanted.

"I don't have to like him," Paula said and put on her teacherly smile.

31

ANDRES OPENED THE DOOR of his car and motioned me in. I was still in my school uniform, a block from Melena's. Every few weeks we'd gone to the white Coppelia tower for ice cream, and he'd lectured on some topic of Revolutionary importance.

That Tuesday the line zigzagged its way halfway down the esplanade. Andres was saying, "We are the first and only free soil in Latin America." He stretched his arm in the direction of the seawall. "Just ninety miles from here . . ."

I counted the metal rings on the fat lady's belt in front of us. Billboard mottoes could be true, but repeating them didn't make them more so.

Still, he went on. "The yankees owned this island. Everything: the electric company, the phone company, the sugar mills. They didn't like a president—" He brushed his hands together twice. "Gone. Nineteen hundred, our poor *mambises* fighting the Spanish with old machetes—here come the yankees, and our name's erased from the history books. *Spanish-American* War." He never raised his voice, but his cheeks were flushed. This was his true passion, his injury: we'd been robbed, left to die. Maybe he was right. Maybe history owed us.

We carried our sundaes past the line to a bench. "This is why I'd give my life to defend this Revolution. Because it's ours. The yankees can't have it." His eyes were shiny with purpose. I suddenly wanted his purpose. Maybe this was what he'd meant by a good fate—righting past wrongs, living for a cause.

He grew quiet, then turned to me. "Look, Tanya"—his voice was low—"I'm not here in an official capacity. I'm here because you need guidance. Unfortunate, but your mother can't provide it." I scooted a little away from him; I needed to see his face. "She could bring both of you a lot of trouble."

I didn't disagree. But I didn't need my personal problems spelled out for me. Like Mamá, I didn't want my strain to show.

"Now it's your turn to be honest with me." Andres bent forward and looked me in the eyes. "Tanya, are you involved in your mother's activities?" He waited. If I said no I'd clear myself but give away Mamá; if I said yes I'd sink us both. Andres said, "If you are involved, I won't do anything, *comprendes?* But you should know that your mother's actions lead nowhere." He opened his eyes wide when he said this. He didn't look so handsome anymore.

Once, in my mind, I'd given up Mamá to Yemayá, ruler of that sea Mamá was so bent on crossing to start life. But one thing was to give her up to an open-armed saint, another to hand her to state security.

I could feel Andres move on the bench beside me. I waited, thinking, "He'll touch me now. Now."

I looked up but he was gone, walking off to his parked car.

It wasn't until later that night, while staring at Cachita's altar in the moonlit parlor—Ochún, goddess of love, looking down in pity at her drowning fishermen—that I understood Andres had come to warn me. He didn't need me to hand over Mamá. He knew. They all knew. Maybe he'd even be the one to arrest her.

32

MAMÁ SAT SMOKING on the edge of the bare mattress. Clothes, blankets, pillows covered the floor. I stepped on them to make my way across the room.

Behind a candle Mamá had lined up more wineglasses full of water. In one was a silver Jesus dunked headfirst to the waist, his shadow enormous on the back wall. I saw Mamá'd written a new note to the saints and tucked it carefully under the glass of the soaking crucifix.

I said, "He knows everything."

Mamá's skinny, long body, usually full at the hips, still sagged a little from her month of bread and *café*. She stubbed out her cigarette in a saucer, stood and then picked up clothes from the floor. She slipped on panties and a bra streaked white on the underarms with dried bicarbonate paste.

"He asked if I was involved in your activities."

Mamá looked up. "And what did you say?"

"Nothing."

"Well. That told him everything." She opened the shutters, then closed them. "It's still dark. Get ready."

"I'm not coming with you."

Mamá took in air, furious, then sat on the bed to strap on her sandals. "Suit yourself. I'm beyond caring now. If he walked through that door, handcuffed me and took me away forever you'd stand by your little man, no?"

I turned toward the hall but she started to pace and rant, and I stayed put and listened to her insults. I wanted to know if she was really going this time, really leaving us for good.

"I'll slash my wrists before I go back to their fucking jail. You hear? That's what Nicolás said. He said they'd send me back to that lunatic bin. You were there. You heard him. Of course you heard him, you *caused* all this. You and your mule friend who stole from me and turned Nicolás against me."

"You're crazy."

Mamá took a step toward me, hand raised.

I walked away and left her there. She shouted after me, "You think you're making progress? Rising up in the world?"

In the courtyard I stood next to Fyor under the brightening sky. Some faraway rooster crowed. Day was coming on.

33

On the early bus to the hilly *barrio* of El Cerro, an old man sat across the aisle holding a grimy canvas bag between his legs—probably on the lookout, like me, for a deal, for something to buy without ration books. The old man's eyes sat wide apart, fishlike, in his head. He winked. "Two more stops," the driver warned me. The old man's fish eye winked again.

The few two-storied houses on St. Paul Street rose weather-beaten out of their dirt yards and tilted a little with the incline. Paper bags and yellowed newspapers flew in the breeze or gathered on the wrought-iron fences. Along the sides of the taller houses, cement stairs led to upper apartments. I went to the last house on the block and headed up the steps.

Were these the steps to my fate? The door opened and a frowning Andres pulled me into a dim, dingy parlor and snapped the lock. I backed myself to his rocking chair and sat. Two leather *taburete* chairs leaned against the far wall, one streaked with water stains. On the coffee table a gold-fish swam back and forth inside a round bowl.

Andres stood over me. "*Bueno.* What was it that couldn't wait? I have to go to work."

This must have been Eleggua's joke on me, on everyone. Eleggua, king of all roads, didn't trick you if he couldn't watch. He'd sat on my bus in his beggar costume and winked his fish eye at me. Now here he was again, in the fishbowl, swimming round and round, his all-seeing black eyes in his slippery golden head.

"What is it? Where's your mother?"

I did what I came to do. "Mamá's crazy. I'm sick of talking about my mother."

A dim lamp shone in the corner. Andres's voice softened. "Tanya." He squatted in front of me and pushed my hair from my eyes. I fell forward and he hugged me to him. I rested my head on his shoulder. "Tanya," he repeated, "you're too young for all this. You're a child." He talked and I clung to him, eyes shut.

But Andres didn't kiss me. I opened my eyes and he was watching me, still concerned, like a doctor.

Was Carina lying when she said men jumped at the chance? Didn't a woman wink and they stood ready, unzipped, waving their stiff things around like battle flags?

Andres picked up the black receiver and dialed. He was tied up, he told someone. He'd get to the office by noon. "We'll have breakfast on the way," he said to me.

"I didn't come here for breakfast." I couldn't tell him I'd come to give myself to a fate. Or worse, that I was like Mamá after all—desperate for my life to start.

On top of the TV sat a picture of Andres and a girl at a beach. "Your girlfriend?" I pointed.

"My sister." He took my hand. "Listen, Tanya. That's how I see you—as a little sister. I want to protect you. I'd never take advantage of you or your situation."

I yanked my hand away. Who said anything about taking advantage? Men were stupid and vain.

34

I STAYED with Andres all day.

He drove me to his office and introduced me to the cafeteria crew as his niece. While he hammered out reports upstairs, I played Parcheesi with the cooks, stuffing my face with lemon ice cream and spicy flour croquettes that stuck to the roof of my mouth. When Andres finished we went to a movie at the Rex and hated the picture— Andres because it had no "seriousness of purpose," me because I couldn't stand Russians bursting into song for no reason. They looked like grinning llamas, big-toothed and full of spit. Andres's elbow brushed my arm in the dark once and I shivered.

Afterward we parked near the Moya and Andres took my hand. "I care about you, Tanya. Please remember that." I thought he was going to cry. His fingers were icy. "Don't worry about your mother." I got out of the car and walked on the cobbled street, feeling his eyes on me. My skin was warm all over.

When I got home I found Melena dreaming on the

couch, her eyelids moving, watching things as she dreamed. Each day she must have woken expecting to see, shocked again that she could not.

The mantel clock read half past ten. I tiptoed past her to our bedroom and threw myself, still dressed, on my cot. In the morning the old lady shook me awake. She said nothing, then woke Emanuel too, repeating his name softly until he opened his eyes. It was the twenty-third, the day of my brother's conservatory exam.

We'd bought him pound cake for breakfast, and my brother dipped long strips into his *café con leche*, slurping until Melena told him to eat silently, "like people." She pursed her lips in my direction and I knew soon she'd tear into me. When Emanuel went to warm up at the piano, she barked at me, "On this day, the most important day in that boy's life, you keep hotel hours? And your mother? Well! She glitters in her absence." The old lady slapped the wood table. "Your brother doesn't deserve this."

This was one of the few times Melena referred to Emanuel as my brother. Most times she called him Manuelito, the name she'd given him. When Mamá or I neglected him, which was probably too often, the old lady stood by him, ready to show him that only she would do right by him. "Blood only goes so far, *mi niño*," she'd say to him. "As you can well see." This was no lie, but it irked me that she propped herself up by rubbing his wound.

But I saw her pride too. She wanted us to acknowledge what she'd done for my brother — how she'd shaped his life, saved it even, because no one else cared and no one else would.

"I'm sorry," I lied. "I was at Paula's."

Melena wiped her hands on her apron. "Go see if your mother's awake."

I went slowly; I didn't want to look. Mamá's door was locked. Her room was quiet inside, dark below the door.

"She's gone to work," I yelled back to Melena, hoping that saying it would somehow make it true. Valentin shouted, "Work work work!" The parakeets shrieked.

I didn't want to think about where Mamá might be, or with whom. I didn't want to worry the old lady on Emanuel's big day. Maybe in the afternoon we'd find Mamá in the parlor smoking, as always, and she'd ask about Emanuel's exam. I wanted this to happen.

Back in the kitchen Melena was at the sink, holding on to the edge as if she were about to fall. Her face was pale. I came up to her and she brushed me away with the flick of her wrist. "*Niña,* the owner's eye fattens the horse so let me tell you something: You're *not* to be running around the streets at all hours of the night like nobody cares about you. Because somebody does." She tapped her chest and squinted, trying to focus on my face with her moist blind eyes. "You're not Paula. You don't have to run around with *machos* to—"

"Paula doesn't do that."

Melena's face reddened. "Paula's your friend, I receive her in my home, but you two are not the same. If boys want to see you, you bring them here. To *your own house.* With all the lights on like decent folks." The old lady closed her eyes for a second as if exhausted, then picked up a dishrag.

Melena was wrong, unfair about Paula. But I saw what the old lady offered me and was moved. I loved Melena; still, I couldn't accept. Maybe I wasn't cut out to be an adoptee. Or maybe I was of my mother's clan: unpredictable, selfish. A slippery heart. Either way, the old lady deserved better.

By noon we were back from the conservatory. Emanuel had passed his exam and now he couldn't sit still. He seemed to buzz inside himself as if a bee flew around in his chest. He told me a Pepito joke making the rounds at school, then laughed at the punch line and repeated it when I didn't laugh too.

"Shut up," I said. I went to Mamá's room and put my ear to her silent door. Emanuel pressed his hand next to mine. His breath still stank a little from that morning when, from nerves, he'd thrown up his expensive pound cake in the conservatory bushes.

"Mamá's been skipping work," I said to him now. "I didn't tell you before because of your exam." My brother's face was still round, with long, soft eyelashes. He stood, suddenly serious, his hands at his side. "Look," I said, "don't worry. You'll be out of here soon."

"You never tell me shit. Like I'm not even your brother," he yelled back and I saw that, despite the old lady's speeches, he still believed in blood ties.

"I'm sorry," I said. And I was. I always left him out of my wars with Mamá. It was a rule I followed. Now I saw I'd done him no good.

Emanuel and I, we should have stuck together like survivors of a storm. But we never did. Instead we got weaker, easy to divide with Mamá's pull and Melena's tug. For a minute I felt that this, not Mamá's troubles, was the saddest thing about our lives.

Finally I said, "Mamá—she's involved with some people, some friends of El Gambao. She's thinking of leaving the country again." Emanuel's eyes widened. "Calm down. She's not gone yet. I don't think."

He opened his lips to say something. Then he walked up to Mamá's locked door and shook the immovable knob. The door rattled. He let go and we put our ears to it again, but there was no sound.

That night Emanuel and I forced Mamá's lock with a knife and found the room as she'd left it two mornings earlier, except she'd taken her note to the saints with her. We walked around the mess as if we were in a crime scene, touching nothing.

Melena came in behind us and made us kneel by Mamá's bed to say the rosary. She handed us clothes from the floor. "We must hold something that belongs to her," she said. "The Virgin is very good at finding the missing."

I went to bed with the drone of Melena's and Emanuel's Hail Marys and Glory Be's in my head. I woke up early, in panic, thinking of the homework I hadn't done, until the night came back to me and I lay sweating, watching the room take shape through the half light of the morning.

When I got up I called Paula and she answered breathless. She'd be at Melena's by noon, she promised, and hung up before I could explain much. But lunchtime came and Paula didn't show.

I was waiting for her on the stoop when Andres drove up. The Moya domino players and CDR gossips stared as we drove off. He said, "I know about your mother."

He touched my shoulder. He said he'd called hospitals and train stations. "It's been a hard day. Let's go somewhere quiet. To talk."

It was a long, beautiful drive down palm-lined avenues to Santa Maria Beach. The brilliant sky and sea air coming in the windows made the world seem hopeful. They made me wish I lived in a somber, landlocked city where I could grieve right for my disappeared mother, my sad brother, for the blind old lady calling me in to dinner as she must have been doing right about now, a helpful CDR member whispering to her that I'd run off with the Stiff Little Clerk— *si, ese mismo, compañera,* the one who sent away Nelita and parceled out your house. And the old lady would shut her door and kick me out of her heart for good.

On the empty beach the light was almost gone and the sand was cool against my legs. We sat side by side under a palm tree. The fronds above us rustled with the wind but the sound got lost in the whoosh of the waves sliding up the sand. Fireflies flashed and flitted by. The sky was filling up with stars.

"I was born in a little town," Andres said. "South of here. Close to Bejucal. Never saw the sea till I was ten. My father died and we moved here, to the city." He looked at me. "I like the sea."

"It scares me," I said.

He smiled. "It's dangerous, but it's a part of us on such a small island." Like Mamá, Andres often talked of the size and shape of our country as if they were harsh, unfair blows against it. But I could tell he liked the island being small and needy — he liked having something to protect.

His eyes were bright. His head moved closer to mine and I panicked and looked away. "Don't be scared," he said. He took my chin and turned it to face him. He whispered, "We're nothing. Life is nothing really." His lips brushed my cheek, my nose, my eyes, and I reached up and held him because what he said was true.

He mumbled and stroked my hair. We kissed with our tongues and he slipped his hands under my blouse. I closed my eyes and ears and opened my mouth to him like Eleggua taking in water, breathing through it.

Panties down to my ankles, Andres said I was too young, it wasn't right, but I held on to his wrists. I hadn't come this far to play everything-but games.

He broke free of my grip and licked my belly, then between my legs. I grabbed his head to push him off — it was embarrassing — but he wouldn't budge. It tickled at first, finally it didn't. He went faster. I raised my butt in the air.

Something in me was breaking and spilling and I'd never get it back. I tried to hold it but it rushed out, lost like breath in the salt air.

There was nothing waiting in me anymore. Now all of me was in the world.

35

A WEEK and two days passed and no word from Mamá. No word from Paula either. I called her house at all hours but she never picked up. Maybe her pearly nails were too wet to answer the phone.

I spent my nights at Andres's now. Each morning I woke before dawn and cried against his pillow. Then I got up wobbly and fuzzy-brained, and made us breakfast. Andres refused to buy on the black market, so most days we had old toasted bread and sugar water. We ate in the kitchen, standing, Andres in a hurry and me trying to avoid Eleggua's accusing fish eye from the parlor. I knew I deserved his stare, for betraying Melena, and for wishing, in some corner of my mind, to be free of my own mother.

On the night I'd come home from the beach in the early hours, belly glazed with Andres's goop, Melena said nothing. She stayed silent the next day as I bundled up some clothes to take back to Andres's apartment. But on my way out she and Emanuel cut me off at the kitchen door. She said, "You're on the fast road to perdition, *niña*. Like your mother. Nobody can stop you. But let's get this clear: if you walk through that door, don't ever come back."

Emanuel looked at his shoes.

Nobody wanted me to stay but Fyor. In the courtyard I kissed his old head and he strained against his leash to follow me out the gate. But I walked away from him too. Leaving wasn't so hard, I saw, even when somebody needed you. You simply stepped out and the world swallowed you up in its glare and clatter and it was over. What you left behind—people, things—never caught up with you again. There was power in this, a kind of thrill. It must have been what Mamá felt each time she ran off.

Late Tuesday morning Ruth Pendestal called Andres and told him Melena needed to see me right away. I dressed and rushed out the door. I thought the worst had already happened: Mamá face down in a ditch, Mamá washed up on the shore, eyes open, unblinking in the sun.

I walked inside the old lady's dark house without knocking. She sat upright on the sofa as if awaiting a formal visitor. "Join us, *niña*," she said, Emanuel next to her, eyes puffy and red. "There's been a phone call from Cáceres."

Emanuel interrupted. "Abuelita Carmen wants us to go there. Fast. She said fast." He wiped his nose with the back of his hand. "She didn't say why."

We both knew Abuelita didn't call for little things. The closest phone was in Elsa's *bodega*, a good ten-minute walk down a rocky path. The times we'd seen Abuelita speak into it she'd held the receiver as if it were a small sleeping animal that could wake and bite her. In the years we'd lived in the city she'd called us twice.

"We don't know if your mother is in Cáceres or not," Melena said. "In any case Manuelito can't run off to the country to track her down. His final conservatory interview is in four days. He's worked his whole life for this."

So had Melena, of course, but I said nothing. Emanuel looked to me.

"She's our mother." I repeated Paula's words about Carina. I wasn't sure I meant them, but I thought my brother deserved a chance to choose.

"A mother acts like one," Melena said.

I couldn't disagree and Emanuel slumped back, relieved. All along he'd wanted me to let him off the hook.

We sat silent in the parlor. Outside rain had fallen and drenched the streets. Children were getting soaked splashing in the deep potholes.

"If I can't find Mamá, I'll be back in three days," I said finally.

Melena said, "Nobody's telling you to go to Cáceres, niña. Nobody is asking you to."

"I'll call you from Elsa's," I said to Emanuel. He nodded. I walked over and hugged him. His cheek was hot and smooth, and his curls smelled of boy sweat.

The old lady sat on the couch. Rain trickled behind her onto the glistening street.

36

BEFORE I LEFT, I went to Paula's to pick a fight. Since Mamá'd disappeared, Paula had never come to see me. She hadn't even called.

I wanted to yell at her, to end our friendship. Then I wanted her to talk me out of that, and out of going to Cáceres too.

Paula's door was ajar. The living room was empty. The white Italian sofa, the plastic table, even the curtains were gone, ripped from their metal rods. At first I thought Paula had moved without telling me, but her wedding picture lay face up on the white tiles; deep cracks on the glass crisscrossed Paula's and Leandro's smiling faces. The plaster on the far wall was pocked and the rocks that had damaged it lay scattered on the floor. Across the wall in bright red paint were the words COUNTERREVOLUTIONARY, GUSANO.

In the bedroom I heard someone open and close drawers. Loló, lit cigar in hand, appeared in the doorway. "Long time no see, *chiquita*." Carina peered around his shoulder.

She took a step forward but he lifted his hand and stopped her. Her face was creased, her eyes teary.

"Where's Paula?" I said.

Carina looked down. Loló cleared his throat. "I asked you the same thing once," he said to me. "Remember?"

"Where is your daughter?" I screamed at Carina. She looked at me, her eyes large. I turned to Loló.

"I don't know where she is." He looked at me, confused. For once Paula's troubles were probably not his doing. "You'd better go now, *chiquita*, and give my regards to your lovely mother."

I smelled steak and onions sizzling as I ran up the steps to Andres's kitchen. When I opened the door he pinned me to the wall and we did it right there, me standing on my tippy toes, knees shaking from the strain. When we fell to the floor I was so full of him, so sad and grateful, I sobbed. He held me and said he loved me. He said we'd get married when I turned sixteen. We'd have children one day and work and study. We'd have nothing to worry about: the Revolution provided for everyone.

"I went to see my friend Paula. She wasn't there. Her place was trashed." I looked up at him. "Paula hasn't done anything."

He gave me his ministry look—cool and suspicious, all-knowing. "She lives alone?"

"She's married to Leandro Pino. His father heads some import-export division."

Andres played with the steak on his plate. Finally he said, "There's been talk of a case at the office." He pulled me onto his lap. "I'm not allowed"—he took my fingers in his—"I'm not allowed to discuss details. All I can say is your friend's fine. I understand Carlos Pino's family was sent abroad. Your friend's father-in-law has been detained—"

"What for?"

"What did I just say?" He slapped my fingers softly, then gave me a mock frown as if I were a naughty child. "I'm not allowed to discuss details." He paused. "Your friend is fine. That I guarantee you."

"But she's gone," I yelled. "And she didn't do anything. If someone said anything against her, it's a lie."

Andres took my chin in his hand. "The family got sent abroad for their own protection. You saw what happened to their apartment. It's better that your friend's not here to face the stigma and the indignation of her compañeros. The family was sent off out of mercy, out of consideration. Carlos Pino did a very serious thing. He placed his family in peril. Worse, he placed the Revolution in peril. Now he'll have to answer for it."

We sat silent. Paula was abroad just as she'd wanted. Andres loved me. Mamá was gone. But each wish granted brought with it troubles I'd never foreseen.

Andres slid me from his lap. "Let's get some fresh air."

Outside the night was cool and the clouds were low and thick. The wind smelled of rain.

We drove along Infanta Street toward the seawall and at a red light Andres put his arm around me. I slid across the seat to him. The rain had started again and a couple crossed the street in front of us, the man holding his jacket over the woman's head.

"Last night my grandmother called from the interior," I said finally. "She called Emanuel. She wants me to come for a few days. She didn't say why." I waited, but Andres said nothing. "Maybe Mamá's there. I have to go see."

"We'll both go," he said.

I cleared my throat. "I know I said Mamá's screws are a little loose, but . . . what if she just wants to leave? You said once that some people can't be dragged along."

Andres slid his glasses up the bridge of his nose. The traffic light changed. He pulled his arm away and placed his hands on the steering wheel. "You're upset about your friend. We'll talk about this tomorrow."

"But maybe Mamá just wants to leave . . . Maybe we should let her."

Andres looked to the road. "The Revolution doesn't hold anyone against his will. Your mother can apply for an exit visa—"

"That takes years. And sometimes the CDR takes away your ration books while you wait."

He looked at me. "Tanya, do you honestly want me to approve of people dying in the middle of the ocean?"

We sat silent. Then Andres shook his head and suddenly turned the wheel to the right and pulled up to the curb. "I'm a fool." He paused. "You know where your mother is, if she hasn't left already. You've always known. You arranged it with her." He turned off the car. "I thought I was seducing you. I actually felt guilty — corrupter of a minor."

"I don't know what you're talking about. Abuelita called last night—"

He grabbed my wrist. His face was inches from mine. "Your mother was going to be arrested. It was a matter of hours. I warned you because I wanted to salvage *you, your* chance at a future." His voice rose. "I could have gotten myself into a deep hole if somebody knew I'd told you. I could have lost everything. I risked that for you. You come to my place and throw yourself at me. Then you tell me your mother is crazy, and then she's disappeared and I swallow that too."

Andres let go of my wrist and his eyes half closed.

"You listen to me," I said. He stared out the windshield. "I don't know where Mamá is." He didn't move. "You and me—that has nothing to do with her. When I get back we—"

"That's not how it works, *amor*," Andres took off his glasses and rubbed his eyes. "You can't just break the rules and start fresh tomorrow. That's not how it works."

Suddenly he looked sad and old. I could have told him I was committed to him and the Party. I could have gone off with him to find my mother and have her locked up for good. But I would not. It was like before, with Mamá, all the times she wanted to enlist me in her escape plans. Some part of me wouldn't budge. Why should it have to, it said. Why shouldn't I keep something, some last bit of me for myself?

"I'm not leaving with my mother—if I find her. I'm coming back. To be with you."

He leaned over and kissed me but then he pushed me back. "I'll take you to Melena's now."

"I want to go back to your place."

"It's over, Tanya. I'll take you to Melena's."

"Don't bother." I got out and slammed the door. The rain plastered my skirt to my legs. A truck rumbled past me and was gone. I ran and the houses flew by me, dark from the latest blackout. Finally I reached the Moya, its roof shiny with the rain.

37

I LEFT THE CITY the next day, a stifling June morning, one week and three days after Mamá had disappeared. By then her room had been stripped of everything but the smell of old smoke. Cachita and Pilar had scrubbed down the walls with ammonia, polished the furniture, washed the curtains, boiled the sheets, mopped the floors, left the windows open at night, but the smell of smoke stayed trapped in the air. Pilar and her baby—it was their room now—would never be rid of it. For this, I was glad.

No one saw me off at the station. Emanuel's final conservatory interview was that morning and Melena, even if she would have left my brother's side, could never have found her way back to the house without help.

Despite everything, she hadn't turned me away after I'd come from Andres's car, drenched and out of breath. That night Emanuel set up my cot in the parlor. There was plenty of room, now that Ochún and the costumed dolls had been moved into Pilar's room. The piano was back in its old place by the window. In the morning Fyor came and licked my face. For a moment it was as if I'd never left.

And yet I had. I was almost a guest now, someone passing through.

Melena asked me to call off my trip. "What are you going out there to find?" she asked. "What is it you need to know you haven't been told?"

"Somebody has to go," I mumbled. "I'm the one with no future to ruin."

"Is that what you think?" Melena's face lit up and I knew she had me. "You throw away everything that's given to you as if it weren't good enough. Like your mother. You have no faith. Our Lord said it, Blessed are those who believe without seeing."

It made me a little queasy. Mamá and me—splinters from the same unblessed stick.

My train traveled east through smoky sugar mills and shoddy *bohios* in the thick green light of palm trees and banana groves. I was too nervous to sleep. I thought of Andres, of his dark dingy house, his old mattress sagging under our bodies. The train stopped in small towns and we stood in line at fly-infested croquette stands before reboarding. At every stop I thought of crossing the tracks and taking the next train back to Andres.

Eight hours later I was in Agüeros, in Cáceres Valley, stomach growling and achy from the bad food. I crossed the street to the old plaza. Spanish street lamps that hadn't given off light for years surrounded the square. The sun had slipped behind the hills and a dull golden light covered the peaks of the Sierra. People, mostly couples, paced up and down the street. I dropped my duffel bag, the one Mamá had once filled with baby pictures and bottles of water for our trip across the Gulf, and sat on the bench beneath the bus sign. Across by the rusted storefront of La Milagrosa Cafeteria, a fat man in his undershirt watched me.

"Pardon me, if I may," he said, walking over. "If *la señorita* is waiting for a bus, maybe I can assist her." I shook my head and pulled my duffel bag up to my lap. He bowed slightly. "I'm Ocuna. I'm here to pick you up, *señorita*. Your mother, Mirella, sent me." My heart jumped.

The man was dark-skinned and had a long nose. Several front teeth were missing. A scraggly kid walked up to me and tried to grab the duffel bag. "This is my nephew, Eladio," he said. I held on to the bag.

"Where is my mother?"

"If you'll please follow me I'll take you to her. We'll be there shortly."

It was just like Mamá to send a toothless stranger with old-time manners to pick me up. I followed him and his nephew down the darkening streets until the road narrowed to a rutted dirt path leading to the brush. The far mountains mingled with their own shadows in the fading light.

I dropped the duffel bag. "Where are we going?" I said to Ocuna. Eladio ran into the undergrowth.

The pale yellow moon rose from behind the bushes. Eladio reappeared, reins in hand, pulling a brown horse hitched to a four-wheeled wagon.

"The ride will take a few hours," Ocuna said. I picked up my bag, threw it in back and climbed up.

Despite the wobble of the wagon on the rocky path and

the creak of the old wheels, Ocuna snored in his seat. I curled up on the dung-reeking hay, my duffel bag in front of me.

For the first time since I'd left the train my stomach relaxed. Hard, bright stars filled the sky. Crickets roared in the still, open country. What did I know of people like Ocuna and his nephew? What if I'd spent my life in the bushes among *majás,* noisy crickets, an occasional wolf? What kind of person would I have become?

And yet, Mamá had sprung from a place like this. She'd leaped from it like a bouncing toad, landing here and there, each time in a worse spot from which she leaped again. And again.

I drifted off to sleep and when I woke, my clothes were moist with dew. The air thundered but there were no clouds. We had reached the sea.

We made our way on foot down another path, pushing apart tall grasses and slipping down steep, sandy terrain until I saw a cabin, like an afterthought in front of the deserted, sharp dogtooth rocks.

The shack's gray wood was rotting in places. The walls creaked with the strong, constant wind. Ocuna knocked three times and the front door opened.

Someone grabbed my head. I knew the feeling of that hand in my hair. In the darkness I felt for Mamá's neck, as on the day she came down from the mountains. Her throat rustled as it did then, with words and laughter — cooing, bright. Irresistible.

38

THAT NIGHT Mamá and I and her five compatriots—rafters did not call themselves *compañeros*—slept side by side on burlap sacks that smelled spicy and sweet like molasses. Teresa Amador was the only other woman. The rest were Ocuna, two fishermen brothers, Romulo and Martín, and Nestor—a Regla teacher and friend of El Gambao's.

In the morning Mamá, Teresa Amador and I carried a card table and two folding chairs outside to the rocks, where we fished and gathered crabs. The men went to town to get the last supplies. The next day they expected the arrival of the raft, a "bin-ban" actually, a boat of metal parts welded together. A friend of Eladio's father, a former Party member from Sagua La Grande, had sold his house for five thousand pesos on the black market and paid an old man to make him this boat. He needed five or six people so the bin-ban wouldn't float too high on the water.

"If I see another grunt after this I'll puke," Mamá said, pulling a gray, skinny fish up from the water. I caught nothing all day. At times strange, green unrecognizable things got snared in my line and I returned them to the sea.

Teresa Amador teased me. Her black hair fell below her waist and she said it was promised to Ochún. "Five years ago I offered it to the Virgin," she said to me, "when my son was drafted. I knew then we'd never get a permit to leave. He got married last May." She sighed. "He's with the system. He knows better, but what can he do? They have to live, he and his wife. That's what happens with children. They slip away from you." She held her hand out, palm up. "I'm going to reunite with my husband in New Jersey. Or die trying." Mamá glared. Teresa smiled at her. "We made a pact before you came not to talk about death."

I could not miss the change in Mamá. Here, with Teresa and the men, Mamá at last seemed to belong. Here she wasn't strange, colorful or seductive. She followed rules, cooked and served without complaint and took her turn washing the dishes in the wood basin behind the cabin. She lined up the plates carefully, scrubbed each one with a rag.

The men were respectful too, and well-mannered. They seemed to understand Mamá, shared with her some obsession or grief that drove them to sail ninety miles north on raging waters. If they ever reached the other shore, half dead from thirst and hunger, they'd have left the old miseries behind. Whether they exchanged them for new ones wouldn't matter. I thought Mamá and the rafters demanded to choose their own brand of suffering. In this they already seemed free.

Mamá was different with me too. "I better learn to like it," she said, watching the sea. She rubbed my arm, the back of my neck, leaned against me as we sat on the windy rocks. And I saw she was scared, faking a calm she didn't feel.

She combed her fingers through her hair. A few gray hairs sprouted unevenly at her temples. Mamá could be beautiful when she looked off like that, searching and full of hope, to the horizon.

"I can't come with you," I said.

She asked if there was someone else I'd rather stay with.

"No. Not anymore."

"Teresa tells me this has to be your decision or I'd never forgive myself. Still, I thought you should come out and see." Mamá paused. She threw a shell into the water below. "*Frijolito*, this is a tough road. It's very risky. I don't blame you. I haven't always been the best mother."

She'd never admitted this and I let myself hear nothing else for a while.

"You shouldn't do this for me but for yourself," she said. "For a chance at a future." I was almost ready to believe her and then I thought of Andres's "necessary steps" to a bright, beautiful future. I didn't want to hear about promising golden futures. "Sometimes we have to take a risk," Mamá said. "To become who we're meant to be."

I told her no one should have to risk death to become who they're meant to be.

She turned to me, "Truth is, some people do. Many people. Depends how lucky you are."

I wanted to keep her talking. It was rare to hear what she really thought without drama or hysterics. "But how do you know it's better somewhere else?" I asked. "You don't know what those yankees do, how they live."

"You read too much propaganda. The yankees are people, like you and me. They just watch color television." She smiled at me. "Neighborhood spy committees, maximum leaders . . . This is no revolution. This is the same mumbo-jumbo we've had for centuries. It sits on my chest, all of it. I can't go on like this."

I tried but couldn't feel such a burden. Maybe I didn't know enough history. Buildings collapsed and rations ran out and Party members took more than their share. Still, I wasn't willing to pay such a high price for a change of scenery. But for the first time I felt there might be something wrong with me since I couldn't see, as Mamá did, all we were missing, and all that was waiting beyond the horizon.

Was my heart small, petty? When I looked in my heart —which wasn't often—it seemed more bottomless than Mamá's ocean. If I fell in, I knew I'd never come back up for air. Mamá rose and walked to the edge of the small cliff. Her hair blew across her face.

"What about Emanuel?" I said.

Mamá rocked slightly, then hugged her sides. "I called him from the village on the day you arrived—that's how I knew to send Ocuna for you. Your brother sounded happy. He passed his interview; he's going to the conservatory. I couldn't . . . I let him get too attached to the old lady. It was a mistake." She paused. "Once I'm in the States I'll send for him. He'll come then. That conservatory's dirty, rundown, the pianos are old. In the States, your brother can study with the best teachers, have the best lessons. The old lady won't begrudge him that."

Five or six seagulls coasted toward the shore. They

dipped their wings in search of food. After a while Mamá's back rose and fell. Beneath the birds' squawks I heard her sob.

The rest of that day I wrote letters on Teresa's pink paper. I wrote to Emanuel, to Melena, Paula and Abuelita Carmen. (I started one to Andres but ripped it up.) I told them Mamá was leaving soon. I said she was determined, and I'd stay to see her off. To Emanuel Mamá wrote separately. On the sealed envelope above the address she scribbled, "For my son." When I was done with my letters I gave them to Ocuna to take to his nephew's in the village. I kept my letter to Paula—I had no idea where to send it—and drew on it a picture of the rocks, the cabin, the roaring sea.

I'd once heard a girl at school, a Jehovah's Witness, talk about a kind of baptism where you go underwater out of choice and come out changed, committed somehow to a new life. The girl whispered this to a possible recruit, though it hardly ever worked—everyone knew Jehovah's Witnesses gave up birthdays and dancing, wore old-lady skirts, flunked out for missing Saturday classes or were picked up by state security and thrown in jail. But I remembered this girl now because it was possible that I too was getting baptized by a set of loonies and would never be the same again.

At mealtime the men came back with the final provisions. Nestor, the schoolteacher, lit a cigarette and looked at my picture on Paula's letter. "Why is the sea so angry?" he asked me. The waves on the letter were tall and spiky.

Nestor was the leader. He wasn't tall or handsome, but

he had a clear straight manner and as a teacher was used to giving commands and following through. He wasn't much older than Andres and when he put his arm around my shoulders, I winced. "I have a fifteen-year-old daughter like you," he said, "but on the other side." He nodded to the sea.

The men had brought provisions from Eladio's — ten jugs of water, sugar, crackers, powdered milk, cans of sardines, hard-boiled eggs, alcohol and mercurochrome. I was sure everything had cost plenty on the black market and wondered how Mamá paid for her share. The bin-ban would arrive the next afternoon and they'd all leave at dawn before the sun was high and the griffin security boats began patrolling the choppy waters of nearby Baconao. It was agreed if a griffin picked them up they'd never reveal how they'd gotten their materials or provisions in case others escaped and wanted to try again. They repeated the rules: the women were lookouts, the men would row in shifts. Nestor spread a map on the ground and outlined the route to a place named Cay Sal Bank. The yankee Coast Guard was most likely to spot them there. But only the brothers Romulo and Martín had really trained for the voyage, spending whole nights on an inner tube pretending to fish while studying the griffins' surveillance schedule and trying to overcome their fear of sharks. No one else knew anything about the sea. Teresa could barely swim.

Nestor saved the good news for the end: the Party man, Roque, who had bought the bin-ban, had now secured a '56 Chevy motor.

"A motor." Mamá sat up. She grabbed my hand. "A

motor. It'll get us there safe and in half the time." She paused. "This changes everything." I recognized the frenzied tone of her old voice and it scared me.

Nestor spoke. "Eladio's decided to come too."

"I'm telling my father tonight," Eladio said. He and Ocuna seemed proud.

Mamá looked up at me. Her eyes shone. "Look at that kid. So much younger than you, and he's decided to go for a better life. He has more sense—"

"Sense!" I said. "What sense does drowning make?"

Mamá stood. She said to Nestor, "We're in."

"Who the hell is 'we'?" I asked.

"I'm your mother," she said quietly. "And I can still speak for you."

Just before evening the truck arrived with the bin-ban, but it wasn't the sturdy welded boat that was promised. It was only slightly better than a raft, as long as an outstretched man. A wooden frame of inner tubes was bolted to two oil drums that had been turned into pontoons. Their welded pointed heads would cut the waves. The Chevy motor sprouted colored wires. When Martín tested it, it coughed like an old man. Nestor said they'd row at first and start the motor far from the coast so as not to attract a griffin. I didn't think he had much to worry about. The motor would never work.

Roque was a short red-faced fellow who gave orders no one obeyed except his young wife, who scurried about after him, a seven-year-old boy following behind. When he wasn't clinging to her, the boy played alone with sticks and shells. His face was pale and he never looked at the sea.

For the next hour Martín and Romulo tested the raft on the water—it floated—and Eladio came with food and provisions. His father would not let him join the rafters and now the boy cried against Ocuna's chest. I looked at Mamá—here was a sane, loving father for you. But she frowned. Maybe she saw it differently—here was a good son who did as his father asked. Ocuna put his arm around Eladio and softly slapped his nephew's back. "Your day will come, boy," he said. "We'll see each other soon."

That night I packed my duffel bag and left it in the bushes behind the cabin. I would go back to the city. Right before dawn Mamá and the others would wake and plunge themselves into the ocean and I'd never see Mamá again, even if she lived. So despite myself, I stayed. I would see her off.

But outside Ocuna screamed at Roque — hadn't they kicked him out of the Party for being a moron? Nestor said to us, "The raft was transported here on a stolen vehicle. It's not safe to wait. The militia will look for the truck and find us soon. We have to sail. Now."

"In the pitch of night?" Teresa said.

Mamá grabbed my shoulder hard. Her nails clawed me and I shook her loose.

Ocuna and Roque sized each other up. Ocuna was at least five inches taller. The Party man's eyes were fierce. Nestor stepped between them. "People, there's no time for this."

Martín and Romulo, Ocuna, Nestor, Teresa and the provisions were in the bin-ban when we heard the first siren, far in the distance. The Party man worked himself down the rocks before his son, holding him as the boy latched on to a rope someone had tied to the stolen truck's fender. "Don't look down," his father told him. It wasn't too far to the raft, maybe two meters, but the boy was scared. Roque's wife went behind the boy, silent, her big eyes open and unfocused.

Mamá turned to me. "I'm going back now," I said.

"Back to what?" She scrunched her face. I thought this was how she'd look in old age, if she lived that long. She shouted, "Hear that siren? Where do you think you're going to go? That's the police."

Below on the bin-ban, Roque cursed me. Nestor yelled, "We don't have time, *niña*. Come down now or step aside and let the others through."

I saw in Mamá's face she wouldn't give me up. She'd already given up Emanuel. Roque still cursed me. The water crashed below me, and the wind shook the branches above Mamá's head. Pine needles floated to the ground.

Mamá turned me around and walked me backward to the edge, gently, and hand over hand, I lowered myself down the rocks, calm at last. I loved Mamá. This was the stupid, dangerous secret I'd kept, mostly from myself.

Below me the faces on the bin-ban rocked in and out of view. The black sea wavered and broke, roaring, splashing against my skin, the water cool on my bare legs.

I held on to the rope. Nestor stretched both hands up and grabbed me by the waist. I closed my eyes and let go.

39

THE MEN took turns rowing. The breeze was steady and the coast lights flashed on and off. The bin-ban pitched left and right in the waves. "Hold on tight," Mamá said next to me, almost cheerful.

After nine or ten tries the motor caught a few hundred yards from shore and the bin-ban rumbled and shook into my bones. Small waves peaked and foamed, and Teresa and the boy leaned over the side and threw up. We went along like this, the two vomiting and the rest of us on our stomachs, silent, holding on to the sides of the frame, our legs piled together in the middle of the bin-ban.

Night at sea was cold and we huddled at the bin-ban's center, shivering, our clothes wet. I had barely slept the night before, but the thought of nodding off terrified me.

By early morning the sun burned off the cold gray haze. The water was brilliant, sparkling with thousands of shiny, transparent jellyfish. They looked like tiny ghost heads, beautiful, pale blue. Teresa and the boy lay spent, eyes closed, the boy's back resting on his mother's stomach. The mother stared at him with her wide, disbelieving eyes.

Mamá sat up by Nestor, humming "La Vie en Rose." She went on long after he told her to quiet down. I was sure we would all pay for her taking life so lightly. The truth was that if we had stayed in our country, not Mamá, not one of us, would have been fed to lions, tortured or starved to death in a dark cell. Even if we got caught now, we wouldn't face a firing squad or a gas oven. But here we were, lost in the ocean where north looked like south and east looked like west — a skinny line dividing sky and water.

We pitched and scooted under the sun until, toward evening, the sky turned red. Nestor, Ocuna and I watched the water. Dark shadows circled under the surface.

"They're dolphins," Nestor said, but I knew they were sharks. I spotted the biggest one and a rough, pale fin broke the surface. Romulo said they'd come every day around this time, five or six in the evening.

More sharks showed — three, four. The sun hung above the horizon and the air was hot, but I felt cold. I could feel my heart hard against my chest. And then, just as they had come, the sharks left, making their way toward the orange sun. Only hours later could I concede they hadn't been too bad. They'd let us take the route we'd chosen, swum alongside and hadn't toppled the raft. In some ways they'd seemed better than humans.

Before our second dawn at sea, at four or five in the morning, the wind picked up and the sky opened with a light rain. Waves rose beside us and slapped the air above our heads. The motor sputtered, then stalled. Romulo shouted to Nestor that water had gotten in the exhaust. He and Martín tried to restart it by touching some blue and red wires together. Nestor nodded and Martín pulled at the choke. The wife and the boy, Mamá, Teresa and I huddled together at the center of the bin-ban.

Lightning jumped out of the black clouds. Chango's bolts lit the sky and water. Someone said, "*Santa Barbara bendita*" and a wave crashed against the right oil drum, lifting it into the air. The raft tipped to the left. I waited for it to level out, but it didn't. We were flipping slowly. Someone screamed, "We're going to die."

Above the racket of the waves and the rain and crisp thunder I heard my full name, Tanya del Carmen Casals Villalta, spoken like a promise. I turned to it and for a second the sea gleamed golden green, the color of the muslin dress Paula had chosen to get married in. My limbs felt heavy, the way they do before sleep, and I watched myself sliding, a Storm Captain going over in a six-foot wave, choking in Yemayá's grip.

Part Three

40

SOMEONE IN THE rescue car said *Florida* and I looked out, expecting gardens—green hills and shoots of gladiolas, bright acres of tulips. I thought I saw their blurry colored pinwheels whiz past our window a second before I passed out again.

Later that morning at Fishermen's Hospital, a white-haired Dominican nurse woke me to change my bandages. She said I'd talked of flowers in my drugged-up sleep.

"Because of the name," I said. "*Florida.*"

"*Ay, mija.*" She laughed. "A Spaniard's fantasy. Looking for the Fountain of Youth in a swamp." She laughed harder and the creases beneath her eyes deepened. "Think he found it?" She finished wrapping gauze around my head. My temples flared.

For three days I stayed in bed, under observation. I'd had a concussion, been unconscious at sea for hours. On the bed next to mine Mamá shed sunburnt skin like a rattlesnake. She left trails of transparent flakes on the sheets when she sat by me, pink like a newborn and naked except for panties and bra. Maybe this was why the doctors—especially a young Puerto Rican intern—watched us closer than they had to.

The old Dominican nurse sat me by the window, blanket over my shoulders. Down in the parking lot men in lab coats slammed car doors, nurses hurried off at the end of their long shifts. Behind me, Mamá turned on the TV, and my ears buzzed. The white beds grew powdery halos like heads of angels and floated off the floor. I stared, quiet. If I was going blind like Melena, I thought I should take in everything I could.

By the third evening the TV stopped hurting my eyes. Mamá's head rolled back and forth in her sleep. I looked at my hands in the blue half-light of the screen. They looked like the hands of a stranger. I knew I didn't deserve to be here—not any more than those on the bin-ban who hadn't been found. But here I was.

My eyes watered and my chest filled with a sweet sadness. I felt thankful, astonished to be alive. If this was a loony swamp, I didn't care. Mamá had said the city was full of us—hundreds who'd crossed the same ocean in homemade contraptions. I wanted to run down the long white hallway and out to the streets to knock on doors, shake hands with survivors. I wanted to shout we'd made it.

The next morning when I woke, Mamá was leaning over me, touching my forehead. I asked to go meet the other rafters. We'd go later, she said, when I felt stronger. The Puerto Rican intern squeezed my foot and told Mamá to walk me up and down the halls twice a day.

41

OUR FIRST HOSPITAL visitors were reporters from Channel 13, *Lo Nuestro*. Mamá let them in our room and, like a party hostess, offered them ice water in tiny paper cups.

A man pulled cables from a large black suitcase, hung them over the end of my bed and aimed his high bright lights on us. A woman with a long neck introduced herself as Alicia Olivera and shook hands with me and Mamá, then pushed a yellow pad onto Mamá's lap and asked her to write down our names and ages.

Mamá handed me the pad without looking, then she answered the reporter's questions, calling her by her first name as if she'd known her for years. "Well, Alicia, we came here for freedom, as you can understand," Mamá said, smiling. "So my daughter could have a better life."

The camera swung over to me, to my bandaged head and purple bruise above my right eye. The lights hurt me.

Mamá told the story of our voyage and rescue on the high seas. I remembered nothing after the raft had flipped. Whenever I tried to, my mind turned dim and I could feel only the pull of a hand lifting me from the waves.

She'd caught me, Mamá told the reporter, by the hair as I slid down into the water, after my head hit one of the oil drums. We'd drifted, she said, the two of us alone on a small bobbing scrap of canvas and inner tubes, me unconscious, my scalp bleeding a little, Mamá holding on, sobbing, hysterical.

Alicia squatted and pushed the mike to Mamá's lips. Mamá leaned forward, her eyes fixed on the camera. Maybe she'd rehearsed this gesture since she was a girl mixing dyes in backwater Cáceres.

"It was a terrible storm," Mamá said. "I couldn't hear my own voice with the roar and thunder of that sea. I looked at Tanya and she didn't stir. Nothing woke her. I prayed to the Virgin of Cobre for the sharks not to eat me, not till I was out cold like her. Not till I was dead." She brushed her hair back with her hand. "The terror of that storm and the giant waves, and my daughter lying next to me, without moving, like she was—" Mamá glanced over to me. "Excuse me." She wiped a tear.

This was high drama, the greatest of our lives. The room was silent. I heard myself breathing.

"When the waves died down, that's when I saw the helicopter and signaled with my shirt." Mamá raised her arms in circular motions as she must have done to the Coast Guard. "And here we are. So grateful to God and the Virgin, and to this country, the greatest in the world." She gave a radiant smile.

And who could blame her? She was a hero. More than that, she'd been right all these years: it was possible to survive a storm on a raft, to reach a new shore and begin again. She'd fought me, the sharks, the stormy sea, and she'd won.

Life—hers and mine—was truly about to start.

Over the next few days we had four interviews, all about the same things—the rescue, the storm, Mamá's gratitude, my busted head. We watched ourselves on the TV, rumpled and shell-shocked like time travelers. The nurses were proud. They clapped when our faces came on and the old Dominican nurse, Ursula Cayos, bought us a picture album labeled "Precious Moments." We filled it with English and Spanish newspaper clippings: MOTHER SAVES DAUGHTER IN SAVAGE OCEAN; MIRACLE AT SEA: A SURVIVOR'S STORY; A MOTHER'S GIFT. Mamá drew red frames around our pictures.

Our last day in the hospital she woke early and sat in my chair by the window. I could almost see her eyes reflected in the windowpane, the fat gray clouds passing through her hair. She turned to me. "Back there in that water, when I pulled you out, it was . . . the greatest thing . . . you understand? The greatest thing I've ever done. Better than giving birth." Her eyes were wet.

I looked at her from my bed. The raft trip had scraped me clean inside, like a beggar who finds he's really a prince or like one of those old-time Italians who discovered the earth was never flat. Nothing I ever felt before could matter now.

"Mamá," I said. "You were right. You were always right."

She pushed her long bangs from her forehead and I saw

her moles and freckles, the ones I'd charted as a kid when I'd imagine strange maps across her skin. I walked over and rested my head in the curve of her neck and shoulder. She put her arms around me. A tightness in my chest fell away and I breathed deep, easy. "You're my daughter, my *frijolito*. I've been trying to tell you . . ."

42

THE SEVILLA GARDENS APARTMENTS in Hialeah rose flat-roofed and bare, the name another flowery joke on newcomers. Lisette—Abuelita Carmen's niece and our only blood relative in Miami—drove us there from the hospital. The building wrapped its three walls around a courtyard like the Moya. But here all was quiet except for the air conditioners whirring in the courtyard. Doors and windows were shut and no one gossiped on the stairs. The place was painted and clean. I missed Paula's self-portraits on her old flaking walls.

Mamá was pleased with number 204. She stood on the tiny balcony overlooking the parking lot and green trash bins, and stared ahead full of hope, the way she'd gazed at the ocean.

"The rent is cheap," Lisette said. "Just right for you." Mamá looked back at her. "Until you get on your feet," Lisette said from the bedroom. We wore the clothes she'd brought us—her loud print skirts and huge T-shirts down to our thighs.

The apartment smelled like mothballs. Small white splotches of fresh plaster covered holes in the walls. Lisette led me to a tiny dark room. "This is where you'll sleep." I pictured a cot and the books I'd buy someday, how I'd line them up on the one high shelf in alphabetical order like Andres did back home. But behind me Lisette laughed. Mamá pulled me out, smiling. "It's a walk-in closet, *mi amor*."

The manager came upstairs and Lisette wrote her name on a check green with palm trees and handed it to him. He gave her two sets of keys and pointed through a window to a parking space next to the trash bins. Mamá thanked Lisette, who shrugged without looking at us. She folded her pad of palm-tree checks and threw them back into her purse.

It was close to evening and little lights flickered on in the halls. "Tomorrow," Lisette said after the manager had gone, "we go downtown, to *Echarés*, and say your father abandoned you." I took a step back toward the wall. Lisette asked, "Is it a lie?"

"What's *Echarés*?" I looked at Mamá.

"HRS," Lisette said and I felt stupid. "Whatever HRS is," I said, "they don't need to know my life."

Lisette clicked her tongue. "Don't be so proud. They'll send you a check and food coupons."

I said if I'd wanted food coupons I'd have stayed in Havana. But Mamá put her hand on my shoulder and said softly, "I don't see the harm, *frijolito*. Like Lisette says, until we get on our feet."

43

IN THE FOYER of the New Granada Hotel, Mrs. Walter-Prado shook both of Mamá's hands. This woman had read about us in the papers and got Lisette's number from Ursula, the old Dominican nurse.

When she'd called, Mrs. Walter-Prado congratulated Mamá on a "brave passage" and said the community needed "uplifting stories" like ours. She was giving a luncheon for the Cuba Liberation League and she invited us to join her as her "personal guests."

Mrs. Walter-Prado was sharp and skinny. Her hair was dyed a shiny jet black and pulled tight into a bun. "Wonderful," she said, shaking Mamá's hand. Her eyes traveled beyond us, taking note of arrivals.

She led us down a hallway into a huge room where our names were written on small folded cards set up on one of the many round tables, napkins rising in stiff white flames beside the cards. A waiter set dishes of rice and chicken before us as people walked up to a podium at the front of the room. With each speech we drank toasts to the sponsors and friends of the Cuba Liberation League. " 'Friends' means they gave more than a thousand dollars," Mamá whispered to me. At one point we stood up with everyone else to applaud Mrs. Walter-Prado, who was said to make "everything possible."

After *flan* and *café*, I followed Mamá to the bathroom. There, in the bright lights and noise of flushing toilets, an old woman handed out tissues and little soaps to the women at the sink. We lathered, rinsed our hands and the woman gave us towels without a word. "It's so bright in here," Mamá said, smiling at her, then leaned forward to study her face in the mirror.

The old woman said, "Don't worry. You two are young. When one is young one wears anything well."

I looked in the mirror. The white skirt and navy blouse I'd picked at Zayres with Lisette looked like a uniform. Mamá's black dress was short and skimpy.

We stepped out to the carpeted lobby and stood by an artificial plant with red flowers. Mrs. Walter-Prado motioned to us to wait. Behind her, women kissed on the cheek and passed us as we stood, half hidden by the plant. Tiny bells chimed and elevator doors slid open out in the hallway. I wondered if Mrs. Walter-Prado had forgotten us.

But suddenly she walked toward us, hands extended. "We must get together again," she told Mamá. "You don't realize it but there's been talk of you in some circles. Your story has power. It reaches people." Mrs. Walter-Prado's eyes rested on me a second. They were small and dark and slightly disapproving. Fine lines creased her cheeks and mouth. The elevator doors chimed again.

Back in our apartment, Mamá explained. "That Mrs. Walter-Prado is a philanthropist. Some rich people are like that. They're philanthropists." I'd never heard the word but she went on. "They like to give things to people like us. People with potential."

We sat on the green carpet. Our furniture was two plastic chairs, a card table, a sofa bed and a cot donated by Lisette's in-laws. Mamá took off her shoes and pantyhose. "Mrs. Walter-Prado asked me what I did in Havana. I told her I'd been assistant to a producer but for political reasons my career was cut short. I said I wanted to get back to this, my lifelong love, TV broadcasting."

I looked at her.

"I know, but what did you want me to say? That I'd stuffed matches into little boxes?" She massaged her right foot. "Here's the best part. Mrs. Walter-Prado said she has a friend, someone she'd introduce me to. Rafael Contreras, head of a TV station. She said she'd be in touch." Mamá crouched on her knees and grabbed my hands eagerly, the way Mrs. Walter-Prado had grabbed hers. "I told you. I told you we'd make it." She lifted me up. I hugged her. "She said our story has power. It reaches people." Mamá put her hands on my shoulders. "It does. Doesn't it? It does."

44

No matter when one requested them, Havana operators only put calls through after midnight. I hadn't heard the phone ring, only Mamá shouting into it. "Bastards. They can't do that to you." She kicked her foot against the kitchen cabinet. "We'll get you out, *mijo*. Don't you worry. We'll get you out. *Si, claro*. Before you turn military age." She listened for a while, forehead against the cupboard, then said, "Just don't do anything crazy. Don't do what we did. It's too dangerous. I almost lost Tanya." Mamá repeated this warning each time we talked to Emanuel.

I stood in my nightgown, leaning against the open bedroom door, waiting. I wanted to hear Emanuel's voice but was scared of what he might tell me. Finally Mamá gave me the receiver.

He had news of Paula. They were in Cyprus, she and Leandro. I had no idea where such a place could be, and Emanuel had no address.

Then he mentioned, almost casually, that there'd been no room for him in the conservatory. "The official word came last week."

"It's because of us," I blurted out. "Because we left. We screwed up everything for you." I realized too late he already knew this. "There's no room this year," he said. "Maybe next time." I saw he wanted to hold on to his version of things.

"It's because of us," I repeated. "Andres did this."

Emanuel yelled suddenly, "I should have left with you. That's all. I don't care who hears this."

Melena took the phone. Her raspy voice choked me up.

"*Niña*. Your brother's disappointed. We just heard. One judge said he'd give Manuelito private lessons and we'll try again, maybe next year . . ."

Emanuel yelled in the background. "I should have left," he said again. He sounded crazy. I'd only made everything worse. Another voice rose and fell too, probably Ruth Pendestal's; it was her phone, her living room at two in the morning.

I felt the utter wrongness of what we'd done. We'd left Emanuel behind with an old blind woman. We'd left him to fend for himself alone. I feared then that Mamá and I wouldn't make it here. Not until we brought Emanuel over and made things right.

The old lady's voice faltered, then she said, "Things change. Things blow over. *Niña*, take care . . ."

The line went dead. I held the receiver for a while, then hung up. Mamá lay smoking on the sofa bed.

"We have to get money for his exit permit," I said to her, though we both knew it could take years for a visa to be granted. "We should hurry. He's counting on us."

"He's counting on me," Mamá said.

I stood there watching her in the dark. I heard newspapers crash one by one against the open hallways outside. I felt too tired to stand and walked to the bedroom and lay down.

In the morning Mamá cried on the phone to Mrs. Walter-Prado. Mamá told her of Emanuel and said she needed a job so she could save up and get him out of that "hellhole." She said she had no one else to turn to.

"You know how it is," Mamá said into the telephone, though I doubted Mrs. Walter-Prado did. She hadn't come on a raft. Mamá said she'd come a few years before, on a Freedom Flight.

They talked a while, Mamá mostly listening and thanking Mrs. Walter-Prado profusely at every turn. When she hung up, Mamá said Mrs. Walter-Prado was arranging an event, a fundraiser for us. She'd invite Señor Rafael Contreras, the TV executive.

"It's the opportunity of a lifetime," Mamá said to me. "See? This could never have happened to us in Cuba."

45

EL GAMBAO DROVE UP in a red Buick convertible, top
down, white leather upholstery, the shiniest car in the
Sevilla Gardens lot. He hugged me and his spicy cologne
traveled up my nose and stayed there. I didn't think of El
Gambao as a father but was glad to see him anyway, as I
would have been glad to see anyone from the old neighborhood.

He kissed Mamá hard on the lips. She laughed and
pushed him away, but I saw they'd pick up where they'd
left off. She told him to lock his car. He shrugged and the
three of us went upstairs arm in arm, like happy drunks.

He'd read about us in Union City, in the Cuban paper,
he said, and he'd hopped on a plane to see us as soon as he
could. "You two are famous." He smiled.

Mamá smiled too and wiggled her painted toes on our
living room floor. I asked him where Union City was. El
Gambao stopped rocking and said I wouldn't like it there.
The place was gray and cold. "You two live in Paradise.
Look at that sky, so blue." He pointed to the window. I

asked what he did in Union City but Mamá shot me a look. "*Frijolito,*" she said, "maybe you should go see your friend in the next building. What's her name?"

"Amparo," I said, surprised. This girl was on my bus to school the two times I'd so far attended, and got off at the building before ours. Mamá had already warned me against her. She'd said Amparo was a street kid, maybe on drugs.

"That's the one," Mamá said.

I headed to the door. My arms and face tingled in the heat. Mamá kissed my head and shut the door behind me.

Downstairs, beyond the lot and the cars, a patch of tall colorless weeds stood almost still. I thought of Andres, of his little island floating defenseless in the clear blue water, swept by ocean breezes year round. He would've laughed at this place of weeds, of mangroves and flat land and the strange airless heat that made you drowsy and desperate. He would never have called it Paradise.

I dozed off in the small open atrium, leaning on the wall below the mailboxes. When I woke the sun was lower. There'd been a face in my dream, first a boy's, then a man's, scraggly and sunburnt, both terrified, drowning in a stormy sea. I started back to 204, eyes swollen from crying in my sleep.

From the top of the stairs, my smiling parents waved.

That first weekend, life with El Gambao was a vacation. In mall fitting rooms Mamá tried on miniskirts and bright bikinis. "I have to show off my legs," she said. I thought her legs were too short, her calves too fat, but I nodded back and gave her outfits thumbs up or down.

From the mall we went to car dealers where El Gambao haggled over cars he had no plans to buy. He grabbed any salesman who spoke Spanish and asked questions and made demands about color, delivery dates, extras like sun-roofs and eight-track players. When he worked the sales-man down to a good price, he walked out satisfied, quiet, holding hands with Mamá across the parking lot.

Mamá was happy now. Often she was tipsy and had the giggles. El Gambao nibbled on her neck and ears in pub-lic, something she'd never allow sober. He had a dozen plastic cards and he used them all at different times, as if afraid to leave one out.

That Sunday we ate a big American breakfast of eggs and toast and drove around Miami's fancy neighborhoods —Brickell, the Grove, past private islands where pink man-sions rose like palaces over the bay. Miami was no Havana —the buildings were flat and the streets sprawled on and on, empty of people—but I saw it had a sort of pastel beauty, scrubbed shiny, polished by money. We found a few open houses and walked into rich people's huge, high-ceilinged white rooms. Mamá pretended we had furniture to fill them. "Here's the place for your wall unit," she said to me and winked.

At the end of the day, after so many chlorine-blue pools, garden gazebos and servants' quarters, we could hardly bear Sevilla Gardens' pea-green carpet, the sad yel-low kitchen. When El Gambao went into the bathroom with the newspaper, Mamá said to me, "I think he's going to help us. He'll give us the exit money for your brother. Maybe even some furniture for this apartment. A nice easy chair, a coffee table, something that matches, so we don't have to live like gypsies." She sighed. Seeing all that wealth had made her lose heart. "But I have to work on him. Most men don't see why they need a house and furniture. What they want is to run around like butterflies. Flower to flower. That's your father for you. *Pata caliente.*" She'd started to call El Gambao my father. "He's really doing well for himself, though," she said with admiration, almost surprise. "A man like him. I don't know if you see it, *frijolito,* but your father is still young and handsome. A man like that can have any woman."

El Gambao came out of the bathroom and opened the Parcheesi box he'd bought me at the mall. We lay on the carpet, facing each other over the game board. Mamá went to the fridge for her box of chocolates. Games bored her. She forgot whose turn it was and lost track of her score.

She sat by El Gambao and stroked his thigh. "You'll drive us to our fundraiser on Tuesday, right?" She leaned close. "You'll get to see us in action."

He took her hand and cleared his throat. "I have to go back up North, Mirella."

Mamá stiffened.

"I'm sorry, *mi vida.* But it's my job. It pays the bills."

Mamá waited, but he never invited her along. She might have ditched Mrs. Walter-Prado's appearance if he had. El Gambao kissed her. "I'll be back as soon as I can, *amor.* You know I'm crazy about you. I love you both." Mamá turned her face from him a little. After a while she kissed him back but her eyes stayed open. An old darkness passed through them, and then was gone.

46

Monday a perfumed box arrived from Jordan Marsh. The two dresses inside—a black one for Mamá, a navy blue one for me—were perfumed too. They were the same color as the dresses we'd worn to Mrs. Walter-Prado's dinner, but the material was soft and slick. "Silk," Mamá said. Inside the box was a handwritten invitation to the monthly meeting of a group of poetesses, the Cuban Lyres. Mrs. Walter-Prado had told Mamá these were "dear people" who'd love to meet us both and help us get "a little head start" in this country.

Mamá said to me, "I'm almost glad your father's not coming to this. Señor Contreras will be there. And your father, sometimes he's very jealous."

The meeting was in an old movie theater in a section of town called Little Havana. Of course it didn't look like Havana, not even a scaled-down version of it, except for the neon signs in Spanish. The poetesses led us onstage, and Mrs. Walter-Prado introduced Mamá as a "true hero-ine and brave mother, an emblem of the strength and courage of the Cuban woman." We sat on folding chairs on the scuffed, dirty stage, made of discolored wood, two large planters of tiny palm trees on each side of us. Mamá crossed her legs at the knee, calm. Her black eyes were bright, rising and falling as she told again the story of our rescue. She told it as if it were her first time, slowing down in places, looking into the darkness.

The lights came up in the theater, and after the applause, we answered questions. Mostly the women fished for compliments: Did I like it here? What did I think of the supermarkets brimming with cereal boxes and cartons of ice cream?

One poetess asked about our family. I said I missed my brother, our old aunt back in Havana, my best friend. I said nothing of Andres. Mamá added I was very happy to live in a free society. The women nodded, but I saw rage well up behind some eyes.

At the reception in the lobby they walked up to us clutching black-and-white photos of their grandchildren wading on Varadero's shore or standing by a statue of Marti. "You remind me of my granddaughter," one said to me. "She's your age now." She shoved a wrinkled photograph into my hand. A skinny girl sitting on a large rock squinted against the light. Another woman said, "That bastard. He's destroyed our families. Bastard."

He was on their lips after that, what he said or thought, and above all, when he was most likely to drop dead. It seemed all Miami prayed for this. We'd been told police drilled on weekends—they'd have to contain the happy crowds the day *he* finally signed off to hell.

Some of the women asked about him as if we knew him, as if he were our personal friend. Was there much support for him in Havana? Did he ever look ill? One of their husbands, an ex-Batista colonel, asked whose fault it was that decent people—he meant himself—had to come die here, away from family, in this free and great and strange land where they would never feel at home.

I couldn't answer him, but Mamá sidestepped the question; she avoided, hinted, then came back to the subject at hand, which was us.

She showed no disappointment, only slight impatience when, toward the end of the night, the crowd dwindled. There was no sign of Contreras. Mamá was no closer to a job or to the six hundred dollars it took for Emanuel's exit request.

I turned to the buffet table, heaped with plates of tiny colorful foods cut into squares and circles and rectangles. Mrs. Walter-Prado stood a few steps behind me saying goodbye to some of the poetesses.

"One thing is to read about this tragedy," one said. "Another to see it firsthand."

Mrs. Walter-Prado said, "We had a good turnout. I was afraid people were still away for the summer. This was something fresh, no?"

I heaped little crustless sandwiches on my plate. For our fresh story, I thought we deserved a good meal.

We got that and more. The rest of the week checks poured in, as well as furniture, clothes, three blow-dryers, a small black-and-white TV. A Cuban-owned agency gave Mamá free driving lessons. Milano's Supermarket sent a letter with coupons for groceries. Our apartment filled with a squeaky dark rocker, two wobbly garden tables, three lounge chairs, a tall vase and a dresser. It was like the days of Loló's bounty—only now we didn't have to hide our profits. Mamá called them "the fruits of our labor."

After a week we took everything we couldn't use to Mario's Thrift Shop. With the money we got there and the checks from the fundraiser, Mamá opened an account at Republic Bank for $335.28. It was more money than we'd ever seen.

Still, it wasn't enough to bring Emanuel here. So we waited to meet Contreras. Mrs. Walter-Prado promised it'd be soon.

47

THE HRS LADY, a Mrs. Lopez, had enrolled me in Hialeah High, a plain two-story beige building several miles from Sevilla Gardens. I'd been terrified my first week but was a little relieved once I heard Spanish spoken in the halls.

By my second week I was sleeping the night through when Mamá had a nightmare. She charged into my bedroom, her hands out like a zombie. I called to her but she was asleep with her eyes open, panting, running from something or someone in her dream. Finally I said "Mirella" and her eyes shifted. She saw me, mumbled something and staggered back to her sofa bed in the living room.

At breakfast I asked about her nightmare but she blinked and said she couldn't remember it. She stirred our *café con leche* on the stove. "Maybe I caught your forgetting disease." She rubbed my head where my raft bruise had been.

"It's not contagious."

"No?" she said. "Maybe it should be."

She went to the dresser to light a candle for our raft compatriots, the ones lost at sea. We'd done this each morning, prayed for their safe arrival, though there was probably no use—no one had been found.

I told Mamá I'd started to remember a kid from our trip, his freckled, terrified face. I dreamed of it sometimes.

"That was the Party man's boy. Ten years old." Mamá walked out to the balcony and stared at the gray morning sky. "And the mother?" she asked. "What about that poor woman? At least she didn't outlive her own son. That, *mija*, would be the cruelest fate of all."

That morning I was late and missed my bus. I had to walk the fifteen blocks to school by the little "doll houses," as Mamá called them, and their shiny lawns. I dodged sprinklers and barking dogs rushing to their fences. A *gringo* dog owner stood by his shrubs, a hose in his hand, and waved to me friendly-like, as if he'd known me all his life.

My school was full of refugees but I couldn't tell them from the Americans. The Cuban girls gave themselves away mostly in PE, leaning against the wire fence, chattering in Spanish. They combed their hair in the wind and took turns swabbing blue eyeshadow on each other's closed lids.

Miss Navarro glared at them. But I knew what these girls were thinking: sweating and jumping in the heat was for monkeys. Or for the lanky freckled *gringuitas* who breezed by them in short shorts and long, tanned legs.

I stayed back with the Cuban girls, still in my street

clothes. "I'm sick today," the girls said to Miss Navarro in chorus, pretending to have their periods.

"You girls are sick every day." Miss Navarro turned away. She blew her whistle and the *gringuitas* flocked to her like a swarm of bright, hardworking bees.

In second period Mrs. Cohen, our English teacher, passed around pictures of her *gringo* husband and their Coca-Cola collection — their fifties bottles, white and red ad signs, an old vending machine they kept on the back porch. Mrs. Cohen wore pressed dark pantsuits and bright scarves and pearl earrings. She sprayed her hair and it stayed fixed in immovable layers.

To collect things was very American, Mrs. Cohen explained to us, and said we should start collections of our own — stamps or baseball cards. When she'd come here from Bogotá twenty years before, she'd collected antique fountain pens. "What *might* you collect?" she asked Amparo beside me. We were practicing the word "might."

"Condoms," Amparo said and put her head back down on the desk.

Mrs. Cohen handed out blank slips of paper we were to hold over our mouths when we repeated "parrot" and "toy" after her. Mrs. Cohen's paper sprang back and forth after each English *p* and *t*. Ours didn't move. Then my paper wiggled outward once and from this little test Mrs. Cohen announced I'd be in regular *gringo* English class by the end of the school year. She said I'd learn the language fast because I was "flexible." My classmates stared at me. I already knew the refugee code — to resist, or appear to resist, becoming a yankee.

"Flexible" sounded to me like a new way of saying I had no convictions. It sounded like Andres's charge against me, that I changed hats easily, with no remorse.

Mrs. Cohen smiled at me. "*Señores,* have a little faith," she said in her polite, careful Spanish. "You'll make it. Why not? I learned English when I was your age."

Amparo slept. Belkis took out her makeup kit. Mrs. Cohen put her chin on her open palm and for the first time I saw disappointment behind her bright look. We were the wrong sort of refugees—lazy, indifferent, disrespectful. We didn't love America and Coca-Cola collections.

"If you do well in high school you can have loans, scholarships. You *might* study anywhere in this country." Belkis kissed a tissue with her purple lips.

"Have a little faith," Mrs. Cohen continued.

I wanted to tell her, faith wasn't the right word. But then she turned to me with her bright, determined eyes, and I saw she wasn't all wrong. So many things could be counted on, on this side of the ocean—well-kept roads, twenty-four-hour electricity, overstocked supermarkets. Faith here might not be such a gamble.

Still, people seemed no better here, only luckier to have landed on the easier side of history. And where was the justice in luck, that it should happen to some and not others? Such luck wasn't worth believing in.

Mrs. Cohen leaned forward. She meant well and I gave her the nod she wanted, though I had no plans to win scholarships and travel this huge country. I had enough strangeness right here to last me a lifetime.

48

AFTER SCHOOL Mamá turned from her Venezuelan soap opera to *Mission Impossible* so I could practice my English. "I won't be summoned with assignments like that white-haired *gringo*." She nodded to Agent Phelps on the screen beyond her feet. "Next time Mrs. Walter-Prado calls, I'll ask for *her* phone number. Then I'll do the summoning."

Dishes lay piled in the kitchen sink, the newspaper spread on the counter. The want ads had been crossed out with a marker, then crumpled in the garbage. Mrs. Walter-Prado had suggested Mamá become a dental assistant. It paid $3.25 an hour, and Mamá could get loans for the course work at a technical college.

I remembered Mrs. Cohen's offer of study loans. Everyone seemed to think borrowing money figured in our future. "I told the old lady," Mamá said, "pardon me, but while I learn to scrape teeth, what does Tanya eat, slices of air? I need a job now. I have to bring over my son." She shook the hair out of her eyes and crushed her cigarette. "You know what Lisette does for a living?" Mamá looked at me. "Fourteen years in this country and she walks the floor of a purse factory. She's a floorlady. She bullies poor people like herself. *That's* what she does."

The deceitful flowery name of Lisette's job struck me. *Flor lady.* I pictured Lisette as an old-time *capataz* lashing slaves in the sugar mills.

"I'm not doing some sorry-ass job for the rest of my life." Mamá exhaled. "As for Contreras, it seems he's the invisible man." She looked away, then smiled. "In the meantime your father'll come through for us. I'm sure. He promised to help with Emanuel."

I opened my English book on my lap. The invisible man and the disappearing father left little to choose from.

Mamá went to the kitchen, then came back and said, "You're not like me about men, are you? I mean, you're no romantic." She put her hand on my arm and I looked up from my homework. "I don't blame you. Look where romance has gotten me." She sat on the couch again. "Your father's crazy. I know that. I love him, OK?" Lately Mamá had taken to saying "OK," the next best thing to learning English.

She let go of my arm. "You never talk about that fellow," she said. "The funny-looking Communist who sent that box of books." He didn't just send me books, I thought. I lived with him. I loved him. I missed him even now.

I stood and went to the bedroom. She followed me, still talking.

"What do you want?" I asked. I was losing patience.

"*Nada.* Only to show you that everybody makes mistakes." Her voice was low. She waited, then said, "You miss Havana. Don't you."

"I miss my brother. I miss the old lady."

"And how do you think I feel?" She grabbed my arm. "Don't you think I cry? I miss him, I miss everything, even the smell of garbage in the old streets. Even Cachita's gruel. I don't get it." She turned to me and took my shoulders. "*Frijolito*. Things aren't so good yet. But we'll give this place a chance, OK?"

"I don't mind the place," I said, and it was true. But I wanted Mamá and me to start work on that life she threw us to the ocean for. I wanted our life to start.

Mamá hugged me, then walked back to the kitchen. "You'll find a job," I said from the bedroom door. She nodded, then plopped two hot dogs in boiling water.

49

AT THE END of October Mamá was hired as a reception-
ist for a Venezuelan import company in the shopping strip
near our apartment. She dressed up in one of the three
dresses she'd bought at Mario's Thrift Shop and some
borrowed stockings from Lisette, and walked there and
back. She managed to keep the job for a week. Things
went well as long as the calls were from Latin America. But
when a district manager heard Mamá's English he let
her go.

Later she took a job as a saleswoman for the Three Sis-
ters Clothing Store in the same strip but got fired the same
day. I never found out why.

Meanwhile Mrs. Cohen had found me a part-time job
in the public library. I was happy there, in the quiet musty
aisles, straightening books. At the end of my first week
Wuthering Heights appeared on my shelving cart, the book
I'd never finished at Melena's, only this time it was the
original version, the actual words someone had written in
a cold English parlor a few hundred years before. I hid
with it behind the encyclopedias.

A blond *gringo* who smoked pot each morning by the school wall pulled up behind me with his full cart. I pretended to shelve the book and he said in English, "It's a library. You can take it home."

That night I lay reading in my room, Spanish/English dictionary next to me in bed. El Gambao had flown in again for the weekend and lay on the couch drinking and watching baseball and fighting with Mamá. "Answer me, *cabrón*," she bleated. "This is your last chance."

At dinner, Mamá, El Gambao and I ate in silence. Finally Mamá said to him, "I asked you a question before."

El Gambao put down his sandwich and closed his eyes for a moment. "Shit. Mirella, for once can we eat in peace?"

Mamá threw herself forward, almost touching El Gambao's greasy chin with the tip of her nose. "I'm supposed to sit around and wait for you forever? Is that it? I'm thirty-five years old. I have fifty dollars to my name. What am I supposed to do when that's gone?"

"You want money?" El Gambao stood up and emptied his pockets. Dollar bills, dimes and quarters flew about the carpet. "Here's some fucking money." The two white pockets hung from his hips.

Mamá's eyes went teary with rage. "You degenerate son of a bitch. All that time in that shithole of a country, wiping our asses with newspaper, not a goddamn letter from you in three years. We took off in a tin can in ten-foot waves. Because you left us. Like dogs. You didn't care if we lived or died." She flapped her hands in his face. El Gambao didn't flinch. "I go out begging, amusing rich women with the pathetic story of my life. Your son is rotting in that hellhole —"

"He's not my son." El Gambao said this calmly.

Mamá pointed to me. "And her? Is she your daughter? Do you support her? Or is she an orphan that we have to beg the *gringo* HRS for charity?"

El Gambao's smile froze. Mamá paused to smell his fear and figure out where it came from.

She took her time. Mamá said she'd given his name and address in Union City to Mrs. Lopez, the HRS lady. I couldn't tell if she was lying.

"Last week. I called her. Now the American courts will be after you." El Gambao rolled up his fingers into fists. Then he strode across the room, kicked the screen door open and stormed out. Mamá followed him.

"Don't you threaten me, woman," he yelled from the parking lot. "I don't like threats." His car door slammed and he drove off.

Mamá marched back into the house and closed the door softly. She looked tired. She was crying. I sat with her on the edge of the sofabed and gave her toilet paper to wipe her nose.

"Why can't he just lend us the money?" I asked.

"It's not that simple." Mamá wouldn't look at me. She blew her nose. "Your father's life is complicated."

My stomach ached. I'd asked the question but now I wanted her to stop talking. She'd started, though, and wouldn't stop.

"I can't keep all his dirty secrets." She paused, then turned to me. "Look. Your father's married, OK? She's a doctor. The money, the business, it's all hers." Mamá paused. "I saw her picture in his wallet. She has the face of a truck driver." Mamá slid her hands down her cheeks. Then she cried out, "*Por Dios! Frijolito,* your father's turned into a gigolo."

I laughed out loud through my stomach pain. I couldn't help it. I ran to the bathroom, locked the door and sat on the edge of the tub trying to catch my breath until I leaned forward, dizzy. I put my head between my knees. The fan whirred in the ceiling and above it I heard Mamá's sobs, and then my own heart beating. Something came to me, something I'd read that day at the library. An Argentinian named Borges wrote that the impulse of all things was to keep being themselves—a stone wants to stay a stone, a tiger, a tiger.

So Mamá, El Gambao and me. Forever ourselves, here, everywhere.

50

MELENA DIED late at night of a stroke. Cachita called with the news. I stood in my huge T-shirt in the dark, holding the phone, listening. "The doctor came and gave your brother something for his nerves," she said. "Emanuel begged me to call you right away. He made me promise. But he's sleeping now. Call him back later, *niña*. Call him later."

Mamá finally stirred after I hung up. I told her the news and she sat up in her sofa bed motionless a long time.

I sat down by her feet and cried, my head on my knees. I felt as if we'd come to the end of something. The old lady was dead, still and quiet in her coffin in some funeral parlor, her blind eyes shut for the last time. I'd deserted her, I'd deserted my brother.

"What's going to happen to Emanuel?" I asked Mamá.

"I don't know how I'm going to live another day," she said. "I don't know why I'm still alive."

I stood and screamed, "You're alive so we can bring Emanuel here."

She looked up at me. "I can't even bring in a few pesos."

"You saved me in the ocean. You can save your son," I said, my voice still loud.

In our bank account was $11.57. All month bills had piled up in the mailbox—the phone bill, the electric bill—and Mamá had torn them up.

The only mail we answered was Emanuel's letters. He never said how scared he was, but his situation was growing worse. Cachita was threatening to sell the piano. The CDR had stepped in and there was talk of sending him to a country school where he'd pick tomatoes in the morning, study in the afternoon, clean latrines at night. These scholarship kids, as they were called, wore pretty uniforms and toted shiny new valises on their weekends home, but they looked hungry, had varicose veins and split nails from field work, and they fell asleep in their classes. Mamá and I again promised Emanuel we'd soon have the money to send for him. We told him to have patience — it was only a matter of weeks. Once we could request the exit visa, we were sure it'd be granted and we'd be together, soon. And here, Mamá promised him, he'd have the best piano lessons, the best music schools, everything he'd ever wished for.

Meanwhile I borrowed rent money from Lisette. Mamá sat in bed with cigarettes, the curtains drawn like at Melena's. Mrs. Walter-Prado's occasional calls stopped when our phone was cut off for nonpayment.

Since their fight Mamá had refused to call or write El Gambao, so I did. At the library I typed his name to show through the window on one of the envelopes enclosed with our bills and inside I stressed the urgency of our "need for communication." He showed up three weeks later, tanned from a vacation in the Bahamas. When she saw him Mamá ran into the bedroom and locked herself in. El Gambao pleaded with her through the door, tried to force the knob. But Mamá never made a sound.

After some time El Gambao turned, pale, and stuffed a bunch of hundred-dollar bills into my hand. "I was waiting till I had this to give her. I know I'm a shit, Mirella," he yelled for her benefit. "I know. I'm *un barco*, but I really love you, *chini*. I love you both, Emanuel too," he said to me. "You're my little girl, the only little girl I'll ever have. Tell her I won this in Nassau. For her." He touched my cheek and left.

"Mamá, please," I called out to her.

She opened the door and we counted nine hundred-dollar bills. I told Mamá we'd file the exit request for Emanuel. I told her I'd pay the rent and the phone. Mamá nodded, then lay on the sofa bed and turned on the TV.

51

A FEW DAYS LATER Mamá put on one of her three dresses and took a bus to Señor Contreras's office. Mrs. Walter-Prado had finally arranged an interview.

I went to my job after school. There, the pothead *gringo* gave me a ride home. He turned out to be Julio Brito from Matanzas, the province named after the slaughter of Indians. The lights in the library blinked for the third time and Julio waited for me by the time clock. He had a surprise outside, he said, and took me to a rusted beige van in the lot. He said his "old man" had come by (his parents were divorced) and given him and his sister guilt money and the use of his van.

We climbed in and sat on the high seats looking down on other cars in the parking lot. Julio leaned over and took my hand. His face was pink in the van's heat and he still looked American to me. He kissed me open-mouthed, his tongue nervous like a lizard's over my shut lips. "What's with you?" I said and pushed him away. Julio started the engine, still smiling.

Back at Sevilla Gardens Mamá's light was on. I let Julio kiss my shoulder, the back of my neck. I remembered Andres, that slight painful tickle I'd get between the legs. Julio held me close against him and kissed my mouth. I kissed him back, his fine dirty hair in my fingers like silt. I knew then we would do it someday and it would be sweet, sweeter than with Andres because Julio wasn't my fate. He was a guy I liked. He was my friend.

When I climbed out of the van Mamá was standing in our building's entrance. She was still dressed from the interview, her hair freshly combed and sprayed.

"That was some farewell," she said, her palm lifted to stop my explanations. "Just ask your little friend if he'll drive us somewhere. I'm sure he will, if you ask him." She grabbed me by the arm. "Don't tell me you're shy all of a sudden. Tell him it's a party. A free dinner." She waved to Julio to wait.

He got down from the driver's seat and walked toward us.

"*Mijo*," Mamá said, "how about dinner at Versailles?" She smiled.

Julio looked at her, then at me.

"It's not his van," I said.

"Mrs. Casals—" he started.

Mamá waved this away. "Oh please. Call me Mirella. May I?" She climbed up. "What a wonderful car. So spacious. How very nice of you, *mijo*. You know, Tanya talks about you all the time." She smiled at me. "Get in, you two," she said. "*Vamos*. Free food. It's not going to kill you."

52

IT TURNED OUT that Mamá had waited all day in Contreras's office but he'd never shown. Mrs. Walter-Prado suggested that Mamá come to the Versailles benefit to catch his attention.

Mamá and I had eaten at the tacky mirrored Versailles several times with El Gambao, but tonight it overflowed with people and a maître d' at the foyer checked invitations. Mamá didn't have one but she spoke her name and the wrinkled maître d' crossed out something on his list. Three *mariachis* in the back pounded out an old macho tearjerker, "I have no throne and no queen / And no one to understand me . . ."

In our jeans and T-shirts Julio and I stuck out among the fancy gold-rimmed Cubans. Mamá pressed forward through the thick crowd and we came to Mrs. Walter-Prado and Alicia, the reporter. Mamá kissed both on the cheek and Alicia, big and long-necked like a goose, looked down at Mamá, trying to place her.

Julio pulled me to the food table. He pressed behind me at times, his breath near my ear, whenever the crowd surged forward from someone pushing his way in or out. At the other end of the room Mamá was now talking to a tall, thick man with graying sideburns.

The man's head was bowed to Mamá's and she was smiling. The crowd shifted and I lost sight of her.

We made it to a corner. A waiter passed with a tray of champagne glasses. I grabbed one and gulped it down. My back was pressed to Julio's chest, his arms crisscrossed around my waist.

The crowd swayed again and we moved back to the wall. Julio took my empty glass. I said, "Let's get out of here," and grabbed his hand to lead him through the crowd.

Outside, a round white moon shone on the car roofs. We walked fast toward his van across the street.

In the parking lot a small wrinkled man appeared in front of us, grinning, reeking of beer and sweat. He touched my arm. A white *guayabera* shirt stuck to his puny chest and shoulders. "Tanya, right?" He extended his hand. "I'd recognize you anywhere. You and your mother. She's looking fine. I saw you two when you came in but I couldn't get close enough to say hello. Too many people. Too hot." He paused. "You don't know me?" His hand dropped to his side.

I'd seen his eyes before, large and terrified. Julio stepped toward the old man, who said to me, "What's wrong with you? You don't recognize me?" He pointed his finger to his chest. "Martín. The fisherman." He talked slower now, as if I didn't speak his language.

"Guy's drunk," Julio said in English.

The man looked around, scanning the lot. "You hit your

head hard. Out. You looked dead." He wiped the sweat from his neck with a handkerchief.

"I'm sorry, I don't remember much after the raft—"

"You hit your head." He punched the side of his head and rolled his eyes.

Julio pulled me by the arm.

"Made it here four months ago. Four months to the day, *niña*. And here I am, parking cars."

"We thought no one survived."

The man tilted his head to one side and cupped his ear.

"We didn't know you'd survived," I said, louder.

He stepped back and studied my face as if the bump to my head had made me crazy. "Your mother called us," he said, offended. "She was very happy we'd made it, me and Nestor, the teacher. He was from your town. From Regla. Remember him?"

A shiver slid up my ribs. He pulled out a set of keys from a hip pocket and threw it to a young man across the lot.

"Mamá called you?"

"I'm surprised, *niña*. I'm surprised you don't know anything."

Julio grabbed my hand and yanked me to the side.

"You saw me hit my head?"

"Out. Out like a light." He blinked. "Like that. Boom. Like dead. You're lucky, understand? *Una reventá.* Excuse me, young man, but that's what your girlfriend here is. *Reventá.* Romulo, my brother, he grabbed you as you went down and hauled you to your mother's tube. The raft came apart, you know, the oil drums, the ropes broke off, everything. Nestor and me grabbed on to another tube.

My brother swam over to us. He was a very good swimmer. But he didn't make it here." He looked to the ground. "He . . . my brother got sick in Dog Rocks. We waited for rescue. It was three days out there. No food. No water." He rubbed his flat stomach. "I'm gaining my weight back now." Martín. The fisherman. He'd shaved his beard and gotten skinny. I recognized him now. "You two were lucky. Your mother said you got picked up right away. We got hauled to some shit camps in the Bahamas. *Reventá,* like I said. My brother, Romulo, he was strong. But he had no luck." His eyes were wet. He pulled a handkerchief from his chest pocket and wiped his forehead and eyelids. "I'm sorry, *jovencitos,* I'm sorry to ruin your *fiesta.*"

"He, your brother, he pulled me—"

The man made a cross in the air with two fingers. "Your mother thanked me when she called. She thanked me for my brother saving your life. Hers too. Why, he saved all our lives. And then there he goes, he's the one that had to . . ."

My eyes watered. He looked at me and said, "*Mi niña,* you leave the tears to the old folks. Be happy you're alive." He touched my shoulder, then glanced around the lot. He said, "We thought you were dead on that raft but here you are." He paused. "To go out on a crazy ocean like that, let me tell you, it takes guts. My brother and me, we were seamen, but your mother, she didn't know. She's a brave woman. You're lucky to have her. *Reventá.*"

Julio stepped toward me and I grabbed hold of his arm. A couple with a valet ticket walked up behind Martín and he led them across the lot. Then he turned and waved and I waved back.

53

Around ten o'clock Mamá walked out of Versailles, hand in hand with the big man she'd been talking to. He moved slowly like a bear.

Julio was asleep in the front seat. I waited for Mamá by the open passenger door.

Martín the fisherman was still out walking around getting cars for people. Mamá went to him and hugged him in the lot. She towered over him in her high heels. He pointed in my direction and Mamá turned and looked across the lot to me. She looked for a long time as Martín talked. She held on to her purse. Then she and the big man walked over.

He wasn't Rafael Contreras but some EFE news executive, Mamá said. I didn't care. She held on to his arm and introduced him as Don Pedro Ortega. "From Murcia." Mamá pronounced a Spaniard's *c* and smiled. The man raised a corner of his mouth a little, pretending amusement. I saw he wanted her.

"This is my famous daughter," Mamá told him. "Look at her." The man turned to me. "Sometimes I can't believe she came out of me. I pinch myself." She pinched her left hand with her right. "But she'll be somebody in this country. Because I brought her here. That's the truth, no?" She looked at me. "You didn't want to come. But I got you out of there. Isn't that right, *frijolito*?" Her eyes were sad but she stood proud and straight. "Now we both start again. We've worked so hard for this and our luck has finally turned. It was all worth it. I was right to get you out. Wasn't I, Tanya?"

There was a slight pang in my chest. Mamá waited, her eyes on me. I remembered Paula's words about Carina, "She is my mother." I remembered what they meant to Paula. I saw they didn't—couldn't—mean the same to me. Still, I tried to honor Mamá, give her her due. She'd brought me from a bad place to a better one. Even in anger, I knew that whether Mamá had actually saved me in the ocean was in the end a technicality.

And yet this one small swindle in a lifetime of swindles stuck in my throat like a fishbone.

"I'm leaving," I told her. "I'm not coming back." I stepped into the van. Mamá turned to the EFE man, her arm raised to him as if to explain. I shut the door and told Julio to drive.

For years I remembered her standing on the side of that street, her right arm up as if in salute, her mouth open in the middle of a word. For years I tried to imagine what that word had been.

But I knew I'd never guess. When it came to Mamá, I'd forever be wrong.

54

THAT NIGHT Julio and I drove by the old Miami River shacks and houseboats bobbing in the dirty water. We drove by neighborhoods with bright green lawns and washed cars.

We could have followed that road, one branch to another, up and away to the California coast. Americans called this their manifest destiny—you left the house you grew up in, the tree in your yard, and never turned back.

But how far could we have run on a small island? Sooner or later all paths lead you in a ragged circle and you spill out to the ocean then, like Mamá, desperate and reckless.

For eight months I lived with Julio, his mother and sister in their two-bedroom house in Hialeah. On graduation we split up—I went off to Boston University on Mrs. Cohen's loans and scholarships, he to Florida State. We always knew we'd split up—or at least I did.

Leaving people and places—once you start, it gets easier.

Mamá found out where I was and a few times she

came and tried to take me back to Sevilla Gardens. She made scenes. But while she was in the hallway screaming, I didn't come out of Julio's room.

Julio asked, "Aren't you too hard on her?" Maybe he was afraid I'd turn on him one day the same way, for some pathetic mistake he couldn't help. "We're all human, no?" he said. I knew he half forgave his old man for taking off with a Honduran waitress when Julio was nine, for dropping in and out, always with a different woman.

Julio's mother sat knitting every night. She said to me once, "Everybody's got sadness. What do you want? A medal?" She went on knitting till her head bobbed and she dragged herself to bed.

I read about a couple who lost their only son in a hit-and-run accident in a small town in Italy, then flew back to donate his organs to the children of that town. I read about a mother who wrote letters to the man who killed her daughter. She pleaded with judges to spare his life. I collected these blessed-be-the-meek stories, and they made me reel with shame. I couldn't forgive myself for not forgiving.

One summer day after graduation, Mamá dropped by Julio's to tell me she'd married the EFE man and they were moving to Spain. I came out to the small, hot living room and sat across from her and wished her luck. We both knew I wouldn't follow her across that new ocean. But we had things to say, and it was best to say them now, before we were both in different cities, the sea between us.

Mamá said Emanuel had called that week. She lit a cigarette. She was still furious I'd left her house, furious I wouldn't see her. So she doled out her information slowly.

Outside the window, the clouds were gone and the sky was the intense, surreal yellow of Florida sunsets.

"Your brother's sending back the exit money," Mamá finally said. She continued with a grim triumphal glare. "Turns out your friend"—she paused for effect—"the crazy Communist with the glasses, found your brother a place in the conservatory after all. Plus room and board at a school nearby. Emanuel's enrolling in the Communist Youth. We're not to write too often, it could hurt his future."

"Why would Andres—?" I stopped. Maybe he had done this to hurt me. But most likely not. Most likely it had nothing to do with me.

"If you don't know why he did it, then who would?" Mamá smiled. She squinted behind her curtain of smoke. "You knew him well, no?"

I walked to the window. "OK," I said. "Enough."

Mamá was ready for this. "Now you say enough. But you'll roast me for my mistakes."

"Look," I said, "we both left Emanuel. He thinks he'll have a future—"

"Fine. I want to give you my address, where we'll be staying for a while in Barcelona."

I took a piece of paper from her.

She grabbed her purse. "I'm sorry I never measured up to your standards."

"Don't go," I said. "I have to tell you something." I paused. "I'm going to college. In Boston."

"Boston." She looked at me, beaming. "I've heard the best English in this country is spoken there."

I couldn't imagine where she'd gotten such an idea.

She took another drag, then put out her cigarette. "I want you to know one thing. Since you moved out, I've gone to the Virgin of Charity Shrine. I've confessed all my sins to the Virgin and to Father Roman. He's given me absolution. He knows what it was like, in that place."

I stiffened and she saw it. "Oh, I know what you think. You think I should have built you two a castle with a tidy fence back in the filth of Old Havana. Or I should have been out each day scouring the streets like a bag lady, or sucking up to some militia man to eke out a few privileges, maybe a few more ounces of rice a month. Is that what I should have lived for?" She paused. "And you blame me for not making it here alone without help. You . . . you wanted the impossible."

"Yes," I said. "So did you."

Mamá looked up, surprised. "I guess I did." She smiled. "I wanted our lives to count. We weren't supposed to count, you know. We never mattered, not to the Communists and probably not to the *gringos* either. But now we're here. I did what I had to do. I made your life count."

She touched my face. I moved forward and she didn't flinch. Her cheek was cool when I kissed it. She walked out to the heat, to the EFE man's silver convertible in the driveway, then waved, her hair blowing back in the wind. I noticed how young she looked, how she filled the air around her. If Mamá had been steadier, grittier, would I have seen the decay of "that place" better, how it crumbled all around us? Would I have blamed it more than I blamed her?

But if the point was love, I loved Mamá most when I

blamed her and fought her to change—to make sense, to work hard on her own for that life she'd promised us, the one she'd always said we deserved.

I feared forgiveness would leave nothing standing, the way a wave erases sand prints. It could come easily, slowly, like the tide sneaking up to the toes. Or suddenly, violently, like a flood.

I knew it would come one day.

And it did.

I fought it. Fought it as hard as I could.